AN INNOCENT IN HIS BED
A virgin—for the taking!

He's a man who takes whatever he pleases—
even if it means bedding an inexperienced
young woman....

With his intense good looks, commanding
presence and unquestionable power, he'll
carefully charm her and entice her into his
bed, where he'll teach her the ways of love—
by giving her the most amazingly sensual
night of her life!

Don't miss any of the exciting stories:

The Cattle Baron's Virgin Wife
Lindsay Armstrong

The Greek Tycoon's Innocent Mistress
Kathryn Ross

Pregnant by the Italian Count
Christina Hollis

Angelo's Captive Virgin
India Grey

Only from Harlequin Presents EXTRA!

KATHRYN ROSS was born in Zambia to an English father and an Irish mother. She was educated in Ireland and England, where she later worked as a professional beauty therapist before becoming a full-time writer.

Most of her childhood was spent in a small village in southern Ireland; she said it was a wonderful place to grow up, surrounded by the spectacular beauty of the Wicklow Mountains and the rugged coastline of the Irish Sea. She feels that living in Ireland first sparked her desire to write; it was so rich in both scenery and warm characters that it literally invited her to put pen to paper.

Kathryn doesn't remember a time when she wasn't scribbling. As a child she wrote adventure stories and a one-act play that won a competition. She became editor of her school magazine, which she said gave her great training for working into the night and meeting deadlines. Happily, ten years later, Harlequin accepted her first book, *Designed with Love,* for publication.

Kathryn loves to travel and seek out exotic locations for her books. She feels it helps her writing to be able to set her scenes against backgrounds that she has visited. Traveling and meeting people also give her great inspiration. That's how all her novels start—she gets a spark of excitement from some incident or conversation and that sets her imagination working. Her characters are always a pastiche of different people she has either met or read about, or would like to meet. She likes being a novelist because she can make things happen—well, most of the time, anyhow. Sometimes her characters take over and do things that surprise even her!

At present Kathryn is working on her next book, and can be found walking her dogs in the Lake District as she thinks about her plots.

THE GREEK TYCOON'S INNOCENT MISTRESS

KATHRYN ROSS

~ AN INNOCENT IN HIS BED ~

TORONTO • NEW YORK • LONDON
AMSTERDAM • PARIS • SYDNEY • HAMBURG
STOCKHOLM • ATHENS • TOKYO • MILAN • MADRID
PRAGUE • WARSAW • BUDAPEST • AUCKLAND

ISBN-13: 978-0-373-82368-0
ISBN-10:   0-373-82368-1

THE GREEK TYCOON'S INNOCENT MISTRESS

First North American Publication 2008.

THE GREEK TYCOON'S
INNOCENT MISTRESS

CHAPTER ONE

NICHOLAS ZENTENAS found his quarry as soon as he stepped into the room. Although the wedding reception was in full swing, the ballroom crowded, he spotted her without difficulty. She was standing slightly apart from the mass of people between the bar area and the dance floor and there was something about her isolation amidst the crowds that drew him.

For a moment he was content to stand just inside the open French windows and observe her. The bright disco lights swirled around the darkness of the room, playing over her long blonde hair and highlighting her in a myriad of different colours that washed over her shapely figure in the long green dress.

She turned slightly and suddenly their eyes connected. He was momentarily taken aback by how beautiful she was. The snapshots taken by his private detective hadn't done her justice.

Their eyes held for what seemed like a long time but was probably only seconds. He felt a sudden fierce buzz of adrenalin. The fact that she was desirable was going to make his task all the more pleasurable.

Cat dropped her eyes from his as her friends returned to her side. She was used to men looking at her but there was something about this man's dark steady gaze that was different. It wasn't just the fact that he was simply gorgeous; it was the way he had looked at her—like a hunter weighing up his prey. She had felt suddenly vulnerable and breathless all at the same time. It was a sensation she had never experienced before and it had left her strangely shaken. Even now, surrounded by the friendly chatter of her colleagues, she could still feel the heavy sensation of her pulse-beat as if it were in tune with the bass of the music pumping around her.

She took a long drink of her water and tried to dismiss the feeling. Maybe she was just hot. London was sweltering in a heatwave and, even though it was nearing midnight and all the doors and windows of the room were open, the temperature had to be around thirty degrees.

Maybe she was also a little too wary of men at the moment, she acknowledged to herself wryly. Recently she had found herself carefully judging every man who spoke to her, wondering if they had been sent by her father or half brother. Crazy really, but the closer she got to her twenty-first birthday the worse these feelings of distrust and anxiety became. Her birthday was now a little under three months away and she couldn't wait for it to pass, she just wanted to get it over with and forget it.

She shouldn't feel like this, she thought sadly. A twenty-first should be something to look forward to, a time of happy family celebrations. If her mother had been alive she felt sure things would be different. But the problem was that the only family she had left was her father and half-brother Michael, and both of them had their minds solely on the money she could inherit if she fulfilled the terms of her grandfather's will and got married before the date of this birthday. She was just a pawn as far as they were concerned. They wanted to move her one step forward towards marriage and then *checkmate,* all the money would come pouring in. Well, she wasn't going to marry for money; she would go to hell before she went along with their plans and she had told them so quite implacably, not that they had paid her any attention.

Why couldn't her father's main concern have been for her happiness—surely it wasn't too much to ask?

The question stirred up the shadows of the past. She felt them inside her now…felt the acute loneliness that had stalked her since childhood. It was amazing how that feeling was never far away, even in a room filled with people. It was the curse of the McKenzie money.

'Hey, Cat, do you fancy dancing?' Some friends caught hold of her on their way towards the dance floor.

Thankful for the interruption to her thoughts, she put her glass down and allowed herself to be drawn along with them out on to the packed floor.

For a while Cat forgot everything and became absorbed by the music. She was here with the rest of the workforce from the advertising company where she had worked for the last three months to celebrate their colleagues Claire and Martin's wedding. The couple had got married in the Caribbean last week and now they were partying in style at this top Knightsbridge hotel. Cat could see them on the centre of the floor, entwined in each other's arms, dancing slowly even though the beat was fast.

That was how love should be, she thought wistfully. Maybe one day she would meet someone who made her feel like that. Someone who loved her, someone she could trust. She had thought that she had meet that person last year. Ryan Malone had been handsome and charming and little by little she had found herself falling under his spell, had started to think that this was the real thing. Then she had discovered that Ryan was in fact a business associate of her brother's and that all he was interested in was wedding her for her inheritance. That discovery still hurt. It had made her more wary than ever about trusting men.

As she turned something made her look distractedly back towards the doors, searching for the man who had been watching her earlier. She had the distinct feeling that his eyes were still on her. He wasn't there and she couldn't see him in the room. She was obviously imagining things. She tried to dismiss the feeling and concentrate on the music but she couldn't get the memory of that dark, broodingly intense gaze out of her mind.

Nicholas watched Cat from his vantage point. She was a good dancer, her movements were lissom and she had a natural rhythm that was very sexy. He had heard it said somewhere that if you were good at dancing you were good at sex. Maybe later he would test that theory; he was looking forward to feeling her move sensuously beneath him. Possessing that curvaceous body was going to be a real pleasure.

However he was deliberately not making a move on her too soon. Instead he was carefully monitoring the situation to see who approached her. He wanted to know if her father or brother had any spies in the camp. He knew they would want to protect their golden heiress. He wouldn't even have put it past them to line up a suitor for her. They had three months to secure the inheritance. He knew that Cat was just as hungry for money as the rest of her family and no doubt the three of them would be determinedly working towards getting their hands on the cash.

Well, Nicholas had different ideas. While he had breath left in his body he wasn't going to allow them to get their hands on that money. He knew it would only be used to wreak more destruction in people's lives.

The very name McKenzie made anger and distaste shoot through his blood like venom from a snake bite. Carter

McKenzie was a snake, he thought acidly, a sly conniving, dishonest reptile. Eight years ago Nicholas had made the mistake of trusting the man with a land deal. Carter had lied to him and dishonestly duped him. As a consequence Nicholas had lost a lot of money trying to put things right, but what really infuriated him was the fact that he had almost lost something far more precious than money. Carter had tried to rob him of his reputation…and had almost succeeded.

It had been a lesson hard learnt. Since then Nicholas had built his own empire and was wealthy beyond his wildest expectations, but he hadn't forgotten his old enemy. He had bided his time, watched and waited from afar. During that time he had noted that Carter McKenzie's son and daughter were exactly the same as their father. Michael McKenzie certainly hadn't broken the mould, he was no more than a con artist, and Catherine… Well, she had financed them through one shady deal after another, was complicit in their greed.

According to his sources, there wasn't a lot of money left in the trust fund that she had been using up until now, and without the rest of the McKenzie inheritance she wouldn't be able to fund them for much longer.

Roll on that day, Nicholas thought now with determination. Because he intended to step in, sweep Catherine McKenzie off her feet and take what was theirs. Carter was going to rue the day he had ever crossed him. Revenge was going to be very sweet.

Cat left the dance floor and with quiet resolution he moved after her, surprised to see that she was heading for the main exit with speed. It was as if she was suddenly running away from something. He lengthened his stride and followed her.

A few minutes later Cat was standing outside in the heat of the night. The London street was strangely deserted; even the doorman who had been on duty at the hotel earlier was gone.

She felt better being away from the crowds. The panic that had gripped her on the dance floor seemed absurd now. Of course there had been no one watching her. Even so, all she wanted to do now was get back to the quiet safety of her flat.

There was a taxi rank across the road and she had thought she would just be able to jump into a cab straight away, but the rank was deserted. A gentle breeze rustled through the trees in the park opposite but apart from that there was an eerie silence. Cat delved into her handbag and took out her phone to call for a taxi. Then she turned to go back into the hotel to wait.

It was as she turned around that she bumped into a youth wearing jeans and a T-shirt. For a moment she thought it was her mistake and was almost about to apologise to him, tell him she hadn't seen him. But then he pushed her hard against the wrought iron railings and grabbed for her handbag and phone. Shock rushed through her as she realized she was being robbed.

Her phone was torn easily from her grasp, but instinctively she held on to the straps of her bag and for a moment a struggle ensued. She had a fleeting glimpse of his face; then the bag was wrenched away and he turned to run. He didn't get very far, a second later he had fallen heavily on the pavement. She heard the thud of his body and then the sound of her phone and the contents of her bag clattering across the concrete.

It was only when a dark shape detached itself from the shadows that she realized someone had tripped him up.

'I wouldn't push my luck if I were you.' A foot landed on the man's wrist as he attempted to pick up her purse. 'The police are on their way.'

The youth didn't need telling twice, he was up on his feet in a second and running away, his footsteps echoing down the empty street.

'Are you all right?' Her rescuer bent to pick up her belongings. Cat noticed distractedly that he sounded calm and that there was a hint of a foreign accent in his deep tone. As he straightened and looked over at her she saw his face clearly in the street light. Dark intense eyes met hers. It was the man who had been watching her earlier.

She guessed that he would be about thirty-two. His hair was raven-dark, thick and straight. He was very handsome but not in a conventional sense, more in a dangerous, hard way. Everything about him, from the molten dark eyes to the sensual curve of his lips, spoke of power and control.

Aware that he was waiting for her to answer him, she hastily pulled herself together. 'Yes, I think so. Thank you for helping me.'

'You shouldn't have fought him for your bag. You could have been hurt,' he told her bluntly. 'Your life is more important than mere possessions.'

He was right. The realization of how much worse this could have been was just starting to sink in. As she reached to take the bag he held out to her, her hand trembled slightly.

'Come on, let's get you inside.' The hard edge in his tone softened slightly, but the arm he placed at her back was firm.

Cat didn't try to pull away; instead she allowed him to guide her back into the light and security of the hotel. There was a strength about him that was almost overwhelming and she was aware of his hand against her skin in a way that stirred up a fierce shiver of tension inside her. It was a feeling she couldn't quite comprehend. After all, she was safe now…wasn't she?

'Mr Zentenas, is everything all right?' A receptionist looked over at them as they stepped into the foyer.

Cat noticed that she knew his name; she also noticed that as he spoke people jumped to attention. The manager of the hotel appeared, the police were phoned and then abruptly she was being swept away from everyone towards the lifts.

'You can wait for the police upstairs in my private suite.'

It wasn't an invitation; it was more of an order. The doors closed and suddenly they were alone in a very confined space.

She glanced across and met his gaze and once more her senses prickled with awareness. It was hard to identify the feelings he stirred inside her. He was generating something deeper than just the usual feeling of wariness she experienced around men.

She couldn't understand why a total stranger should have such a profound effect on her senses. Maybe it was just the fact that he was exceptionally handsome in a dark Mediterranean kind of way. Perhaps it was the way he looked at her as if he were trying to read the secrets of her soul.

He pressed the button for the top floor and there was silence between them as the lift started its ascent.

Nicholas watched as she leaned her head back against the mirrored interior. She looked pale and fragile and young. Her eyes were an almost impossible shade of jade-green as she looked up at him.

She wasn't what he had been expecting, and that threw him. He certainly hadn't imagined for one minute that he would have protective feelings for her. They had struck from nowhere when he had handed back her possessions, and he had been annoyed by the momentary weakness, had shrugged it off with determination. This was Carter McKenzie's daughter, he reminded himself fiercely, and she was well able for anything… He knew for a fact that she was as conniving and sharp as her family. He had read the reports on her and he wouldn't allow himself to be swayed from his mission of revenge by her deceptive air of vulnerability.

Cat took a deep breath and tried to pull herself together. 'This is…er…very kind of you…' She sought to break the silence and the tension.

'It's my pleasure.' The words were silky smooth.

Was it her imagination or was there a cynical edge to his expression, a harsh coldness?

'I saw you at the wedding reception earlier.' Her eyes narrowed as she looked at him now. 'Do you know Martin and Claire?'

'No.'

The nonchalant admission rang alarm bells. Had her first instincts been correct; was he someone her brother had sent to approach her?

'Why were you at the reception?'

'Because, as the owner of this hotel, I can go where I please.'

'Oh! Oh, I see.' Now that she thought about it, the air of authority that surrounded him was blatantly apparent. She felt foolish in the extreme for imagining her brother had sent him. If he owned this hotel he was obviously a very rich and powerful man, not the kind of person to do anyone's bidding.

'I'm Nicholas Zentenas.' He introduced himself smoothly and then searched her face for any sign that the name was familiar to her. Eight years ago he had been her father's business partner and, although he had never met Catherine McKenzie, she could have known his name.

If she did, she didn't betray the fact even by the flicker of an eyelash.

'Cat McKenzie.' She extended her hand towards him.

He hesitated before taking it, but when he did the firm touch of his skin against hers made little shivers of electricity run through her.

Her eyes locked with the coffee darkness of his and she wondered if he could feel the fierce sensual chemistry that swirled between them, or whether it was just in her mind.

Shakily she pulled away from him, glad that the lift doors opened, freeing her from the intensity of the situation.

Nicholas smiled to himself as he followed her out into his suite. So far the evening was going well for him.

Obviously she had no idea who he was.

He'd intended to track her down next week, as he knew her father would be out of the country then and therefore the risk of discovery was smaller. But as soon as his private detective had told him that Cat would be attending a wedding reception at one of his hotels he had brought his plans forward and had flown in from Athens this afternoon.

He was glad he had taken the risk now. Time was of the essence anyway.

The thief striking outside had been most fortuitous. The fact that Cat was so gorgeous he ached to bed her, even more so.

Revenge was going to be so easy.

His fish was hooked; all he had to do now was reel her in.

CHAPTER TWO

His hotel suite was more like a penthouse apartment. Ultra modern in design, it had black terrazzo floors with circular white sofas positioned to take full advantage of the glittering view out across London.

'This is a fabulous place.' Cat walked across towards the window to look out, her gaze taking in the floodlit rooftop garden and the swimming pool.

'Yes, not bad,' Nicholas agreed. But, as he moved to stand next to her, his eyes were on her rather than the view. The green silk material of her dress moulded to the slender curves of her body. She had a very desirable shape—a waist he could probably span with his hands and breasts that were ripe and ready for a man's mouth to explore. The mere thought of having that pleasure made him harden. 'I keep a suite like this at all of my hotels; it serves well for business purposes, although, as I travel so much they are only used on the rarest of occasions.'

'So where do you call home?' She looked up at him curiously.

The name Cat suited her, he thought, she had the intense gold-green eyes of a cat, almond shaped, somehow bewitching. 'I have a house on the island of Crete.'

'You're Greek.' It was an observation rather than a question and he just inclined his head.

'Crete is very beautiful,' Cat reflected softly.

'You've been there?'

'Yes, my grandfather owned a villa just outside Xania and I spent a few family holidays there when I was young.' For a moment she remembered the sparkling beauty of that white mansion overlooking the sea. She had loved her summers there with her grandfather, had felt surrounded by love and happiness. Then the accident had happened and her mother had died. She had been only ten years old but from the day that her father's car had spun out of control on that coast road everything in her life had spun around too. Crete had stopped being a place of happy memories.

Nicholas watched as her face clouded with some dark emotion and for some reason he found himself wanting to reach out to her and soothe the shadows away. 'Have you been back there recently?' he asked softly.

Cat didn't even want to think about her visit there last year. Her father had prevailed upon her to bail her brother out of a business deal that had gone wrong. When she had got there she had discovered that, far from something going wrong, Michael had deliberately set up a very shady deal. It had been an unpleasant episode and a shock to learn how low Michael could stoop. She had spent the week tracing the people he had conned and giving them their money back.

What was that old saying? You can choose your friends but you can't choose your family? She ran a hand distractedly through her hair.

Nicholas saw her brief hesitation, and then she seemed to gather herself together. 'I've no time for holidays these days.'

She hadn't lied, Nicholas noted, she had just skipped over the truth. His sources had told him she had been back to Crete last year to financially back her brother in one of his deals. His private detective had taken photographs of her coolly visiting the victims of the scam to lend her brother more credibility. A little later, with Cat safely back in London, they had cleaned up on an even bigger con. He really needed to remember that, despite her air of delicate vulnerability, she was a true McKenzie, he told himself firmly. They all seemed to have a knack for lying by omission. The reminder strengthened his resolve.

Cat was surprised to notice a harsh glitter in the dark eyes that raked over her now. It made a shiver run through her, as if someone had just walked over her grave.

'You should go back when you get a chance,' he said, turning away.

The lightness of his tone belied that fiercely intense look, making Cat wonder if she had imagined it.

'I'm going to have a whisky. Can I get you a drink?' he asked nonchalantly. 'A brandy, perhaps; they say it's good for shock.'

Of course she had imagined it, she thought, relaxing. 'No, I'm OK, thank you.'

'You're feeling better now, I take it.'

'I feel more embarrassed than anything else.'

'Embarrassed?' One dark eyebrow rose wryly.

'For having caused so much of a fuss. I should have just gone home. Nothing has been stolen from me and the police aren't going to achieve much; the man is long gone.'

'That's not the point. They might catch him and that would save someone else going through a similar ordeal.'

'I suppose so.'

Her eyes followed him contemplatively as he poured himself his drink and then walked back towards her. The dark suit he wore looked expensive; it sat well on his broad-shouldered frame. She couldn't help but notice that he had a very impressive physique; lean and well honed, he gave the impression of someone who could handle himself in any situation.

There was no denying the fact that she found him extremely attractive. But he wasn't her type, she told herself firmly. Too much money and power was a turn-off for her. She had grown up around wealth and she hadn't liked it, hadn't liked the traits it brought out in people. He was probably arrogant—went after what he wanted and always got it. And there was an air of danger about him that made her feel intensely unsure of him.

But he was overwhelmingly handsome; her senses pressed the point as he reached her side. She couldn't ever remember feeling an instant magnetism like this before.

He seemed to be looking at her very intently. Although he wasn't physically touching her, she suddenly felt aware of an intimacy about the situation. She could almost feel his eyes moving over her face, lingering on her lips. Subconsciously she moistened them, her heart starting to thud erratically against her chest.

As his eyes moved lower she felt her breasts tighten against the satin of her dress. It was the weirdest sensation. No matter how sensibly she tried to tell herself that he wasn't her type, her body seemed to be paying no attention whatsoever. The heat of sexual desire was curling inside her with fierce intensity. She wanted him to touch her…kiss her. In fact, more than that, he made her long for an intimacy she had never known before.

She swallowed hard and wrenched her eyes away from him. This was craziness. 'I seem to be taking up a lot of your time.' She hoped she didn't sound as breathless as she felt. 'I wonder how long it will be before the police arrive?'

'It's Friday night and the call wasn't an emergency.' He shrugged.

'Maybe I should just go.' She tried to think sensibly, but she knew it was panic that was driving her. Nicholas Zentenas was having the strangest effect on her and if she stayed around him she might do something she would regret. She opened her bag to take out her mobile phone and, as she did, she noticed that her keys were missing.

'Something wrong?' Nicholas watched impassively as she scrabbled frantically through the contents of her bag.

'My keys aren't here!'

'I picked everything up from the street,' Nicholas said calmly.

'But I'm locked out now! And I don't have a spare key anywhere.'

'Well…let's see… You can get your locks changed first thing tomorrow and in the meantime you can stay here.' He made the offer in a nonchalant, offhand way.

She watched as he took a sip of his drink and put it down on the table beside him. 'That's very kind of you! But I know the hotel is full. Some of my work colleagues tried to book a room here for tonight and there was nothing available.'

He met her eyes directly. 'I meant you could stay here in my suite.'

The quiet invitation sent her senses into overdrive.

There was a long silence and she could almost feel the crackle of electricity that flowed between them. She noticed the way his eyes moved again towards the softness of her lips and her heart thudded unsteadily. What would it feel like to share a bed with this man? To be kissed all over, have his hands touching her intimately? The question made her feel hot inside, it also made her senses do a weird flip with the intense desire to find out the answer.

Hastily she tried to rein in those feelings. Cat was a virgin. She would have liked to say that she had chosen to remain so because she was waiting for the right person to come along, but that wasn't the real reason—the truth was far more complex than that. The truth was that no man had turned her on to the point that she'd wanted to give herself totally to him.

And the one man who had, had turned out to be after her money—thankfully she had discovered this before giving herself to him, but it had been a close call. Now she found it hard to trust anyone.

And yet here she was, in a hotel suite at one in the morning with a total stranger, feeling more aroused by just the way he looked at her than any other man had managed with numerous kisses and caresses. What the hell was she thinking? The question seared through her. She didn't know this man—and, although she didn't think he was in any way connected with her father or Michael, for all she knew he could be married with four children.

'Are you…propositioning me?' She cautiously sought to clarify the situation and he gave her a smile that was slightly mocking.

'I have to admit that from the moment I saw you downstairs in the ballroom I wanted you in my bed.'

The admission made her remember the way he had looked at her across that crowded room. Yes, there had been purpose in his eyes; he had watched her like a predatory male marking his quarry. She had known it at the time, had known it and been turned on by it. The realization suddenly flooded through her consciousness. Those feelings were part of the reason she had felt so afraid, part of the reason she had left the party and the hotel as if pursued by the devil himself.

He reached out a hand and touched her face. It was the most gentle of caresses, his fingers soft as they moved over the creamy smoothness of her skin. Then his hand moved lower to the sensitive cords along the side of her neck as he tipped her chin up.

His eyes raked over her face with an almost hungry possessiveness and she felt an answering pang of desire deep inside.

For the first time in her life she felt like throwing caution to the wind, felt like leaning closer inviting his lips and his hands to take this feeling all the way to its ultimate conclusion. She couldn't understand her reaction. There had been no shortage of boyfriends in her life but she had never felt anything like this before. Even with Ryan she'd had no difficulty in pulling back from making love. Deep down she had sometimes wondered if there might be something wrong with her because she could think so rationally about passion. Now this man—a man she knew nothing about—was stirring all kinds of wild feelings inside her. It was bizarre. It was also deeply worrying. She felt as if she were out of her depth.

With a strict effort of will she forced herself to break the contact with his hand and take a step back from him.

'I don't sleep with strangers.' She held his gaze with difficulty, fighting the demons that were drumming against her heart, insisting she was making a big mistake here.

'Well, then, maybe we should get to know each other…and fast.' There was a dark teasing light in his eyes.

Most women melted when he looked at them; in fact he couldn't remember the last time a woman had given him the brush-off. By contrast Cat held his gaze with an almost fiery determination.

He had to admit he liked that spark in her eyes and he found himself respecting her blunt rebuff.

She raised her chin a little and met his eyes firmly. 'Are you married?'

The sudden question amused him. 'No…not yet.'

'You do have a partner, then?'

He shook his head, a half smile tugging at his lips. 'Why? Are you interested in applying for the position?' He crossed his arms and leaned back against the window frame behind him, watching her with that hooded look of amusement still in his eyes.

'Don't flatter yourself!' She felt a flare of annoyance. She had been right in her first assessment of him. He was arrogantly confident—a man who always got what he wanted when he wanted it. 'I just have a feeling that back home you have a woman in your life who would be deeply unhappy if she knew you were propositioning me tonight.'

'What makes you think that?'

'You are a wealthy…not unattractive businessman who has jetted into the country on business. It doesn't take rocket science to work out that you probably already have a partner and are just looking for a bit of recreational activity to fill a momentary gap.'

'You are very suspicious,' he said quietly. 'And, if you don't mind my saying so, you don't seem to have a very high opinion of wealthy not-unattractive businessmen, do you?' Although the question was asked in a mocking tone, there was enough of a cool serious edge about it to strike a chord inside her.

He was right—she was suspicious. She didn't trust any man easily, which begged the question—why was it taking so much strength to turn him down? Why did she want so badly to feel his lips burn against hers? The question pounded inside her.

'Maybe you are right.' She shrugged and forced herself not to think about that. 'And maybe I was naïve, accompanying you up here to your suite, but I did assume that because you had helped me earlier that your offer was made with chivalrous intentions.' She raised her chin higher.

He smiled. 'Well, just for the record, there is no woman waiting for me in my bed at home.'

She was aware that she was more pleased than she should have been to hear that. She shouldn't have cared, because she wasn't going to sleep with him. When she did choose to divest herself of her virginity it would not be on a one-night stand with a stranger.

'And unfortunately I do have a chivalrous side.' His lips

twisted wryly. 'It's over there.' He nodded towards a door at the far end of the room. 'And it's called the spare bedroom.'

'Oh!' Against her will she found herself liking that lazy, teasing note in his voice.

'So if you would like to avail yourself of it—the offer is still open.'

'Thanks.' She smiled suddenly and it was as if her warmth lit the room.

She had probably practised that look in a mirror, Nicholas reminded himself sharply.

'If I thought the worst of you I'm sorry,' she added softly.

'You mean thinking I was married and looking for some fun on the side?' He shook his head. 'Don't worry about it. I'm not.'

She cringed. 'I really am very grateful for your help tonight.'

The contrition was probably as false as that feigned look of innocence. But she acted the part very well. He could almost believe that she was softness and morality personified and not a money-grabbing witch who had stumped up several thousand pounds to fund a con trick for her brother.

A witch had no right to be this beautiful, he thought distractedly.

The ring of an intercom on a bureau at one side of the room interrupted them. Nicholas walked across to answer it.

'Mr Zentenas, the police are here,' the receptionist informed him.

'Send them up.' He flicked the switch off and glanced over at her.

Something about the bold sensual glitter in his eyes made a shiver run through her, but she wasn't sure if it was a shiver of apprehension or desire. Feeling as she did, she should have been out of here in double-quick time.

Yet the feeling was exciting, a double-edged sword. She would just have to be careful not to sway too close to the blade.

CHAPTER THREE

NICHOLAS listened as she gave her statement to the police and Cat could feel his eyes resting on her and it made the hairs on the back of her neck stand up.

Why did she feel as if he were weighing her up? Why did she feel this constant tug of almost hostile sensuality between them every time their eyes connected?

There was one point when an officer asked her a question and she couldn't even think straight about the incident outside; it seemed to have paled into insignificance next to Nicholas's powerful presence.

He helped her out at that juncture. She noticed that he spoke with the quiet authority of someone who was used to being in command, and the officers treated him with the utmost deference.

'That was probably a complete waste of time,' she reflected a little later as Nicholas came back into the room after showing them out.

'Not necessarily; you gave a good description of your assailant.' He glanced across at her. 'Would you like a nightcap or do you want to turn in?'

The direct question made her heart thump uncomfortably against her ribs.

She wondered if she had made a fool of herself tonight, asking him outright if he were married! She cringed at the memory, and his arrogant rejoinder—*Are you interested in applying for the position?* Very funny, she thought dryly. Although if her father had heard the conversation he would have rubbed his hands together in glee. The thought flicked through her mind with brief amusement that threatened to turn to aching sadness—her father would probably marry her off to the lowest bidder if it meant he and Michael got what they wanted.

'I think I'll just turn in. I'm quite tired.'

He nodded and led her towards the door he had indicated earlier.

The room he showed her into was extremely stylish, dominated by a huge king-sized bed. 'There is a bathroom through to your left.' He indicated the *en suite* bathroom at the other side. 'Make yourself at home.'

'Thank you.' She turned and looked at him. As their eyes met she felt again the fierce tug of attraction rise deep inside her. 'Well, goodnight, then,' she added firmly.

He smiled. 'Goodnight, Cat.'

As Nicholas closed the door behind him he was aware that the evening hadn't gone quite as smoothly as he'd thought, and it wasn't just that she hadn't capitulated and slept with him; it was more than that. It was a bit like hooking what you thought was a small fish on a line only to discover it could pull you off your feet.

He crossed to where he had left his drink and, picking it up, downed the contents in a single gulp. Then he stared sightlessly out at the glittering lights of the city.

For a second he remembered the softness of Cat's skin beneath his fingertips, the way she had looked up at him with sweet fiery warmth. He'd wanted her with an urgency he couldn't remember feeling in a long time, an urgency that hadn't gone away despite the interruptions and her hasty departure to a separate bedroom.

With a frown he put his glass down and reminded himself whom he was dealing with. That episode in Crete last year had been particularly unpleasant. If she got her hands on that inheritance, God alone knew what strokes she and the McKenzie men would pull.

She was very sexy though, he acknowledged with a frown. Dangerously so, with the figure of a siren and those come-to-bed eyes.

But sex wasn't his ultimate goal, he reminded himself firmly. What he wanted was total possession of her and, through her, total revenge on Carter McKenzie. Their inheritance would be sent to some worthy cause—he had one all lined up, an orphanage in Greece. Quite fitting, he thought with a smile.

So he would bide his time about bedding her, he told himself as he switched off the lights and headed for his own room. His intuition told him that if he tried to rush things with Cat she would pull away from his grasp. Nevertheless he was confident that before very long he would have this all wrapped up. She would soon be his for the taking—along with the McKenzie inheritance—and it would be a most satisfactory arrangement.

Cat lay in the large bed and stared up at the ceiling. She could hear Nicholas moving about, switching off lights. Although she felt exhausted, she couldn't sleep; images from the evening were flicking through her mind.

Something wasn't right.

She saw again the man who had tried to steal her handbag, then Nicholas Zentenas making his timely intervention. What had he been doing outside the hotel? she wondered suddenly.

She turned over and pummelled the pillow beneath her head, willing sleep to claim her. Did it matter why he'd been outside? He'd helped her and that was the main thing.

Cat closed her eyes again but this time she could see Nicholas's face clearly. The dark glittering eyes, the sensual curve of his lips. He was very handsome but she couldn't work out what it was about him that gave him that dangerous edge. Maybe it was just that she was scared of the attraction she felt for him. He wasn't the type of man that she wanted.

When she fell for someone, she wanted him to be a nice uncomplicated kind of man. She wanted an ordinary life where she and her partner worked together to achieve their goals. That was her dream. She didn't want wild excesses of money or to get involved with some power-hungry person who lived for his next deal. She had seen that kind of life up close with her father and she didn't want it.

It was a strange coincidence that this man who had helped her and who she was so attracted to was from Crete, a place that held the key to so many emotions inside her.

You should go back, he had suggested lightly. She had returned to Crete to help Michael last year only because she had felt obliged to. It was a familiar scenario. Her father played the guilt card and she found herself dishing out money to Michael—money that had ostensibly been left for her education.

Her half-brother was trouble, Cat thought darkly. But still her father couldn't see it. He adored his only son, blamed any problems he had on the terms of her grandfather's will—on her—on anything except Michael. And, who knew, maybe it was the will that had caused Michael to stray into troubled waters. He had certainly been hurt by it and so had their father. Cat still felt guilty about the way her grandfather had left things, even though logically she knew it was not her fault.

Cat had been ten when she had discovered that she had a

brother. Four months after her mother's funeral, her father had announced he was getting married again to a woman called Julia. He had then coolly introduced Julia's son Michael as his son. Cat had found she had a half-brother only six months younger than she was.

The revelations had shocked her. Julia had been her father's mistress for eleven years, and yet she had never suspected that all had not been well in her parents' marriage.

Her grandfather had been furious and had made it clear to his son that he disapproved of him marrying again so soon.

'She's a gold-digger.' He had practically spat the words out in front of everyone and a heated argument had ensued. 'She's only hung on to you for all these years because you have wrapped her in the luxury of the McKenzie money and now she wants more. But if you marry her she won't get anything more, I'll make sure of that. I'll change my will.'

The words had certainly stirred up a lot of unpleasant feeling. But her father had taken them as an empty threat; after all, he was an only child, how could his father not leave him his inheritance? His marriage to Julia had gone ahead.

In the intervening four years before her grandfather had died, her father had worked very hard to get back into favour with him. So hard in fact that Cat had rarely seen him. He had thrown himself into the family real estate business, making deals and money that he'd thought would impress his father. Some of those deals had slithered close to the edge of what was acceptable. They hadn't been illegal but they hadn't been moral either. At least that was what her grandfather had told her.

Her grandfather had been less than impressed. He had blamed his son's ruthless dealings on Julia. But in fact Julia had been too busy spending money to be interested in how it was made. She hadn't been a particularly bad woman; Cat would certainly never have classified her as the clichéd cruel stepmother. She was just not the maternal type; she wasn't particularly interested in Michael, let alone Cat.

So Cat had grown up in a household where money was plentiful and love non-existent. She had tried to befriend Michael but he had been a sullen and withdrawn child. They had been lonely years. Cat had thought that things couldn't get any worse until, when she'd been fourteen, her grandfather had died.

She remembered the day the will had been read quite clearly. Remembered the extraordinary fury it had unleashed.

Her grandfather had been a very wealthy man. He had left his property in Crete and in London to his son. Then he'd stipulated that the businesses were to be sold and that the money, along with the bulk of the McKenzie fortune was to be placed into trust for Cat. The rest of the money, which had been a small proportion, had been put into accounts for her education. There had been nothing for her half-brother.

At the time it had seemed harsh. Cat remembered naïvely looking over at her brother and saying softly, 'Don't worry, Michael, I'll give you a share of the money when I get it.'

She would never forget the look he had given her; it had been one of pure hatred.

Her father had sold the house in Crete and used the money to try and get the will overturned in a court of law, but he had not been successful. Gerald McKenzie had been deemed sound of mind and she would inherit the McKenzie fortune on her twenty-first birthday but only if she was married. If she were still single on reaching that birthday, the money would stay in trust for her until she was thirty.

Cat's lips twisted as she thought about it. She didn't know why her grandfather had placed such a stipulation in the will. Perhaps he had wanted to further frustrate his son and grandson by protecting Cat and his fortune from their greedy mitts for a bit longer. Whatever the thinking behind it, Cat didn't want the money. In her eyes it was cursed and had already done enough damage. Soon after the last court hearing, her stepmother had walked out on her father. It had been the final lesson on how money could tear people apart; as far as Cat was concerned, it could rot in the bank.

Her father and Michael, however, had other ideas. They had continually harped on about how wrong it was that she should be left everything. And she saw their point—her grandfather should never have left his will like that. It was that guilt which had driven her to open up the accounts supposedly for her education to give the money to Michael. She didn't want it anyway. She had taken a student loan and, with the help of two jobs, had supported herself through university.

Michael, meanwhile, was into property development and had tried his hand at a number of get rich quick schemes. She hadn't realized what kind of schemes they were until last year when she'd had to go to Crete to bail him out. She had been sickened to find out just how he had been using her money.

When she had told him how disgusted she was, a terrible argument had risen up, fueled by Michael's bitterness. He had let it slip that he knew Ryan and that even Ryan thought she was impossible. After that it hadn't taken her long to discover that her romance had been a set-up. The discovery had hurt her deeply and she had immediately ended the relationship.

She hadn't spoken to her brother for months afterwards. But then at Christmas Michael had turned up on the doorstep of her flat, filled with remorse for the things he had said and done.

For her father's sake she had accepted his apology. She'd been glad that the last of the money for her education had been used; at least he couldn't ask for any more.

But now it was three months until her birthday and Michael was starting to call around at her flat again; the air of friendly politeness was slipping and he was starting to mention the money again, getting increasingly desperate, increasingly angry.

Her father had rung her a few weeks ago. *'You did promise Michael half of that inheritance,'* he had reminded her tersely. *'Things haven't been easy for your brother.'*

She had wanted to say, Things haven't been easy for me either, but I've got myself an honest job and I haven't been deceiving people. But she had held her tongue. Criticizing Michael upset her father and led to arguments. It was best to gloss over things and keep them both at a distance. But she had told him categorically that she would not be getting married in the near future so the problem of the inheritance money would be in abeyance for another nine years.

There had been an ominous silence.

She hadn't heard from either of them since. But she had a horrible suspicion that they were up to something. The truth was that Michael had always been able to twist their father around his little finger. And her father probably wanted his share of the inheritance as well.

She tossed and turned in the bed. Her father was as cold and calculating as her half-brother. It was something she kept pushed to the back of her mind, too painful to dwell on and acknowledge.

After her birthday things would calm down again, she told herself soothingly. All she had to do was hold her nerve for another few months and steer clear of any romantic involvements.

But, as she closed her eyes again, a different problem plagued her—the problem of her powerful attraction to Nicholas Zentenas.

She needed to keep her distance from that man, she told herself fiercely. She needed to leave here first thing in the morning and not look back.

* * *

As soon as Cat stepped out of her bedroom the following morning she could hear Nicholas Zentenas's deep tones. He was speaking in rapid Greek and for a moment Cat was transported back to Crete, to the sizzling heat and the days of childhood. She followed the sound through to the lounge and then round a corner, where she found him outside on the terrace.

He was sitting at a table laid for breakfast. A crisp white linen cloth and silverware sparkled in the early morning sun. However, there was no food on the table; instead he had paperwork spread out in front of him and he was talking on his mobile phone. Cat couldn't help thinking that he looked the epitome of a successful businessman in his dark suit, a blue shirt open at the neck.

Behind him, the rooftop view out over the city was even more spectacular by day. She could see the green swathe of St James's Park and the blue curve of the River Thames.

Nicholas glanced up and their eyes locked. Although she tried not to acknowledge it, she could feel the instant attraction and desire firing her body with a wave of heat. She noticed that his eyes drifted almost lazily to linger on her lips, making her feel even hotter inside.

He smiled and indicated that she should take a seat in the chair opposite his. Cat, however, did not move from the doorway. She intended to wait until he had finished his call, thank him politely for his hospitality and then make a swift exit. She needed to get out of here. The warning bells that had been ringing through her consciousness all night were clamouring insistently now.

As he talked his eyes moved from her face and hair, down over her body as if he were undressing her. She felt a lick of heat deep inside.

Hastily she looked away and tried to pretend that she was

studying the swimming pool and the terrace, but she was aware that his eyes were still on her.

She felt out of place in her silk evening dress, as if she had been summoned like a lady of the night for his pleasure.

Abruptly he ended his phone call. Cat understood enough Greek to know he had promised to ring whoever it was back.

'Forgive my manners, Cat. That was an important business call.' He switched to speaking English with fluent ease. 'How did you sleep last night?'

The polite tone contradicted the way he had been looking at her, making her wonder if she had imagined that raw sensuality.

'Very well, thank you,' she lied with a smile. In truth her troubled thoughts had kept her awake until the early hours.

He indicated the seat opposite his again. 'Join me and have some breakfast.'

'Actually I won't, if you don't mind,' she said firmly. 'I have to organize a locksmith so I can get back into my flat, so I thought I'd head straight off.'

'Pity—I wanted to ask you a little about Goldstein Advertising. You work for them, don't you?'

'Yes.' She frowned. 'How do you know that?'

'It wasn't such a hard deduction; most of the people at the wedding party last night work there.'

'I suppose they do.' She was nonplussed at this sudden turn in the conversation. 'Why are you interested in Goldstein Advertising?'

'Why is any businessman interested in advertising?' He fixed her with a wry look. She was very suspicious and the barriers he had sensed around her last night seemed to be raised even higher. Why was that? Maybe she had been involved in so many dishonest deals with her brother and father that she naturally assumed everyone was as crooked as she was?

'A company called Mondellio handled my last campaign,'

he continued nonchalantly. 'Maybe you saw it; it featured some of my hotels in the Caribbean—the tag line was "Relax in style".

Was that his chain of hotels? Cat's eyes widened. She was impressed; everyone in the advertising world knew that campaign. It had been huge and the envy of all its competitors. 'Yes, I saw the ads; they were good. Mondellio are very well thought of in the business.'

'It was successful,' Nicholas continued smoothly. 'But I think it's run its course. I've been considering changing tack this year, switching accounts.'

Cat found her business mind clicking on like an illuminated sign. If she could bring in a large account like the one Nicholas was talking about, it would be a major boost for her career.

A waitress appeared and placed a pot of coffee on the table.

'But if you have to rush off…' Nicholas concluded with a shrug. 'Goldstein was only a passing thought, anyway—'

'No, I have a few minutes.' Cat found herself walking over towards the table, pulling out a chair.

Work-wise, this could be a lucky break. Things hadn't been going too well for her at the office so far. The money wasn't bad but a lot of the pay was structured around bonuses and she had felt frustrated by the fact that accounts were given to favourites—people in the know who networked. She knew that she was the new girl on the block, but she had student loans to pay off and living in London was expensive. She needed an opportunity to show her bosses just what she was capable of and this might just be it.

Nicholas tidied away some of the papers whilst the waitress poured them both coffee. That had been almost too easy, he thought with a smile. The lure of a lucrative deal was something a McKenzie never could resist.

The waitress handed Cat a menu before discreetly withdrawing.

She glanced down at the choice of food but didn't feel like ordering. She couldn't eat anything—not with Nicholas watching her so closely from across the table. Her burst of enthusiasm for work had suddenly been overshadowed by her awareness of him again. Maybe she should have followed her instincts and left. She could have asked him to come into the office on Monday to discuss business.

But then maybe he wouldn't have come, she told herself sensibly. And an opportunity that she badly needed would have been missed.

She frowned and put the menu down. 'So in what way exactly were you thinking of changing tack with your advertising?'

Nicholas noted that instead of trying the hard sell she was making an effort to find out what he wanted. Obviously she had a shrewd business mind. 'Do you want to order some breakfast?' He deliberately ignored her question and glanced down at the menu.

'Actually, Nicholas, I don't eat much in the morning but the coffee is most welcome, thank you.'

He looked over at her in amusement. 'You know the first rule of making a good deal is never to negotiate on an empty stomach.'

'Well, as we are just chatting and I'm not looking to make a business deal, that's all right then.'

The laid-back approach was also impressive.

He glanced over at her with a quizzical light in his dark eyes. 'How long have you worked at Goldstein?'

'Three months.'

'First job since leaving university?' He pretended to hazard a guess.

'First full-time job. I've worked evenings and holidays all the way through university.'

Why had she done that, he wondered, when her grandfather

had set aside more than enough money to fund her education? He took a sip of his coffee. Maybe she had just preferred to speculate with that money on her brother's dirty schemes.

'If you are thinking that I am not capable of handling an account of your company's size then you're wrong,' she said quietly.

'Really.' His lips twitched. Not so blasé now, he thought sardonically.

She sat back in her seat and as their eyes met she found herself having to be honest. 'Actually, the truth is they are confining me to quite small accounts at the moment but I've got lots of fresh new ideas and I could do so much more.' Her eyes sparkled earnestly. 'The fact that I've got so much to prove and you are looking for something different could work in both our favour.'

She had just hooked him back in with a gold star; those big green eyes were very enticing and so was her zesty attitude.

He had to hand it to her; she was a witch of the highest class. Nicholas hesitated and then reached into the pile of papers next to him and passed her a file that Mondellio had sent him. They had set out a few proposals for amendments to the original ad. 'See what you think,' he invited lazily.

Nicholas watched as she leafed through the pages and read selected areas carefully.

Silence stretched between them. He noticed little things about her—the long sooty darkness of her eyelashes and the natural blush of colour along her high cheekbones. She bit down against the softness of her lips with pearly white teeth as she concentrated.

'Well, it's perfectly obvious that this isn't the way to go,' she said at last as she put the file down.

He had expected her to say that, but what he hadn't expected was for her to continue swiftly and identify exactly what the problem was. He was surprised by how insightful she was, but he was stunned when she started to come up with some very novel ideas of her own.

'If you go with this deal it will be modestly successful, but that's all. What you really need is to grab the public's attention all over again.' She flicked the folder closed. 'Obviously I could come up with some ideas if I was given time to work out the details.'

She glanced over at him when he made no reply.

'I may be fresh in at Goldstein but they are an excellent company. With their experience and my new approach you could have a very exciting and successful promotion. Think about it.'

Goldstein was lucky to have her—the grudging light of respect lingered inside him for a moment. She was intelligent, sharp and creative. Pity she was also insincere and corrupt like the rest of her family, he reminded himself quickly.

'But don't think about it too long,' she added with a smile.

He was aware that she had turned the tables on him slightly. When he had set out to get her attention with business this morning, he'd had no real intention of switching accounts. That had just been a piece of bait to cast out before he went back to Mondellio to ask for changes.

Now—well, now he was undecided. He really didn't like Mondellio's proposals. Maybe he would think about Cat's ideas. She was right—Goldstein did have a first-rate reputation and business had to come first after all. Also it had occurred to him that this might be just the excuse he needed to break through those barriers of hers and draw her closer into the net and into his bed.

'You have made some interesting suggestions,' he said. 'Maybe I will want to delve deeper, hear more.'

She tried to draw her eyes away from his, but somehow she couldn't; he held her locked into that powerful gaze. And suddenly her mind was veering away from business towards altogether more risky terrain. Delving deeper had a tantalizing ring about it.

From nowhere she found herself remembering a snatch of their conversation from last night.

I don't sleep with strangers.

Then maybe we should get to know each other…and fast.

She was very glad when the waitress returned to the table. She didn't know why she was thinking again about that conversation; it was embarrassing.

'Can I get you anything else, sir?' the woman interrupted quietly.

Nicholas glanced enquiringly over at Cat and she smiled politely and shook her head.

'No, that will be all, thank you.'

The waitress withdrew and then stood at a discreet distance, waiting and watching in case Nicholas should summon her. His every whim was catered for, Cat thought as she took another sip of her coffee. His days were probably filled with staff dancing attendance and women fawning over his every word. Well, she was glad she hadn't given in to her desires last night, she told herself firmly. She'd just have been another notch on his belt. Sex would mean nothing to him; it would have been merely a passing recreational moment.

You could never trust a man like Nicholas Zentenas. He would look on a woman as no more than a plaything in the bedroom.

But doing business with him—well, that was another thing entirely. She had not missed the gleam of respect in his gaze as she'd told him her ideas and she had got quite a buzz out of it. Business was everything to a man like him. Making money was probably more of a turn-on for him than sex and, as for love… Well, the only thing a man like him would love would be a successful deal.

She had learnt a thing or two about relationships from watching her father.

'If you want to drop into my office some time next week we can talk about my ideas in greater detail,' she invited coolly.

'I'll see how I'm fixed. I've got a pretty hectic schedule lined up.'

Cat allowed the subject to drop. Despite his offhand response, she was quietly confident. She had made her pitch and it had been good; she was content to sit back and wait.

'You certainly started work early.' Her glance moved towards the stack of paperwork he had placed on the empty chair between them.

'I'm in the midst of negotiations to buy another hotel and I'd like to get things wrapped up as soon as possible. Time is money.'

'Well, I'm sure the deal will fly through. You strike me as a man who always gets what he wants,' she said flippantly.

'Not always.' He looked at her and for a moment there was a gleam in his dark eyes. 'But I enjoy a challenge.'

Something about the way he said those words made her tingle inside.

The ring of his mobile cut the silence between them and with a sense of relief Cat pulled her gaze away from his and reached to finish her coffee.

She listened as he answered his phone. It was another business call in his native Greek language. Something was displeasing him; his voice was crisp and authoritative, his look intently serious.

Although Cat couldn't speak Greek fluently, she had picked enough of the language up when she was younger to be able to make a competent stab at it. And she understood it pretty well. Nicholas seemed to be checking on the progress of some building work for an orphanage—no, she must have got that wrong, she decided quickly. He must have said building work for offices; he spoke so quickly that she couldn't catch the details.

After a while Cat found herself tuning out as her eyes moved contemplatively over his features. He just oozed sensuality. Her eyes drifted down towards his lips. What would it feel like to be kissed by him? He would be very experienced, would probably be an incredibly masterful lover… Her heart gave a weird little flip.

He hung up and glanced across at her and with a jolt she realized the errant direction her thoughts had taken.

Gathering her scattered wits together, she pushed her chair back from the table. 'I really should be going,' she said quickly.

'Yes, me too.' He glanced at his watch. 'I'll drop you off,' he offered.

'No, it's OK—'

She supposed it was churlish to refuse but she really did just want to get away from him. She didn't like the effect he had on her one little bit.

'I insist. If you are ready, we'll go. My driver should be outside by now.'

Nicholas led the way through the apartment towards the lift. As soon as he pressed the button, the doors swished open.

'I think the waitress got the wrong impression about us this morning,' Cat remarked as they stepped inside and the doors closed.

'In what way?'

Cat tried not to look embarrassed. 'Because I'm still wearing my clothes from last night, I think she assumed that something was going on between us.'

'Does it bother you what people think?' The deep velvet tone seemed laced with amusement.

'No, not at all!' She held his gaze steadily.

He smiled. 'It's just unfortunate that I have a crystal-clear conscience about last night.'

Something about that smile and that teasing light in his dark eyes made her feel that he was right and it was very unfortunate that last night hadn't gone further.

Hurriedly she looked away from him and told herself to snap out of this. 'It would have been a mistake!' She hadn't meant to say the words aloud; they escaped impulsively and quite vehemently before she realized it.

'Maybe... Maybe not.'

Cat made the error of looking over at him. He really was far too attractive for any woman's peace of mind. 'Well, we will never know now,' she said softly.

'Won't we?'

He countered the question in a tone almost as provocative as the glint in his eyes. That raw sexuality made her want to lean closer, beg him to take her here and now.

He was toying with her, she told herself sensibly, teasing her to gauge her reaction and see how far he could go with her. In reality he wasn't interested in her. And certainly if she had slept with him last night he would be checking his watch and running through his business plans now as if she didn't exist.

Yet, for all those sensible thoughts she ached for him to come closer.

For a moment Nicholas considered reaching out to halt the lift. He could see heat in her eyes and, as his gaze moved over the curves of her figure he found himself imagining how easily her breasts could be freed, her skirt hitched.

The only thing that stopped him was the undercurrent of tension. He sensed that, beneath those sultry smouldering eyes, Cat's defences were still on high alert. The time wasn't right for her surrender to him...but it soon would be.

His lips curved in a mocking smile. 'Maybe we'll test that out some other time when I haven't got such a busy schedule.'

He really was arrogant! The words caused her head to snap up and her eyes to blaze. 'I don't think so.'

He laughed at that.

The lift doors opened into the lobby and she marched out ahead of him.

The normality of the reception area seemed almost unreal after her tumultuous thoughts. He really was the worst kind of man—full of his own importance and far too confident. And he had the worst kind of effect on her. She hated herself for the weakness that invaded her as soon as he was too close.

There was a doorman on duty this morning and he swung the heavy glass doors open for them so they could step out into the brightness of the morning.

The air was buzzing with the sound of the London traffic and there were a few people strolling past, but it was the white Rolls Royce waiting by the kerb that drew Cat's attention. As they walked down the red-carpeted steps, a uniformed chauffeur sprang from the driver's seat and came around to open the back passenger door for them.

'Actually, Nicholas, I won't take a lift with you.' Cat stopped a few paces from the vehicle, the thought of being in a confined space with him for even a few moments longer making her very nervous. 'I've just remembered I have to stop off somewhere.'

'I see.' There was a gleam in his dark eyes as he looked over at her.

Did he see? Did he know that she was running scared? She hated the fact that he might, just as she hated the swirling conflicting emotions he could create inside her.

'There are plenty of taxis at the rank across the road, so I may as well take one.'

'As you wish.'

He sounded vaguely amused now. She tipped her chin a little higher. 'Anyway, thank you for all your help and if you need to discuss those business ideas we talked about earlier, do give me a ring—'

She forced herself to hold her ground a moment longer and opened her purse to take out her business card.

His hand brushed against hers as he took it and she immediately felt a flare of arousal. She found it incomprehensible how just the smallest touch could have that kind of effect on her. Business was the only thing that mattered, she told herself firmly. 'My office number and my mobile number are on there. I'm in from about eight-thirty until six most weekdays.'

Nicholas smiled. 'I'll give that some thought.'

She watched as he coolly tucked the card into his jacket pocket.

She would probably never see him again. The thought was disappointing—but only because it would be a business opportunity lost, she told herself quickly.

'See you some time, then.' With a cool smile, she turned away.

CHAPTER FOUR

THE office was crowded and airless and Cat was not having a good day. In fact it had not been a good week. Her immediate boss had overlooked her again and handed out two lucrative contracts elsewhere.

'Sorry about that, Cat; you did come a close second,' Victoria said smoothly as she brought the meeting to a close. 'But I feel I've got to play safe. This is an old and valued client and it's experience that counts at the end of the day.'

'Well, it's your decision to make,' Cat said as she started to fold away her presentation. What else could she say? Anything else would sound like sour grapes. But inside she was fizzing. Especially as the contract had been given to a man Victoria was rumoured to be having an affair with—a man whose pitch had been the least exciting of the afternoon. Cat hated gossip and paid no heed to it usually but she really was starting to wonder if there was something in the stories now.

One of the receptionists put her head around the door, interrupting the general feeling of unrest in the room. 'Cat, there is someone downstairs to see you.'

Cat's heart sank even further. She assumed it was her brother; he'd phoned three times this week and she had avoided him on each occasion. It would be typical of him to barge into the office and try to create a scene. Her nerves stretched; she really could do without that! No one here knew about the situation with her family because it wasn't something she liked to discuss. In fact, when anyone questioned her about her background she always pretended everything was fine in her life and that she was close to her father and brother. The truth was too sad to acknowledge and too embarrassing. For one thing, she would have men mockingly asking her to marry them if they knew about the inheritance!

'It's not my brother, is it?' she asked cautiously. 'Because I'm too busy for personal matters, you'll have to tell him—'

'No. This is business.' Judy cut across her swiftly. 'His name is Nicholas Zentenas—owner of the Zentenas chain of hotels.'

Cat's wasn't the only head that swivelled around towards the door. Judy had everyone's attention now.

'He was Mondellio's client,' someone remarked quickly. 'Isn't he that Greek tycoon? Remember that huge campaign—*Relax in style*?'

There was an excited buzz around the room.

'So what is he doing here?' Victoria cut across the noise sharply, her eyes boring into Cat. 'And why is he asking to speak to you?'

'I ran a few ideas by him last week.' Cat tried to keep her voice nonchalant but inside her heart was starting to speed up. A full week had passed since she had given Nicholas her card. She had hoped every day that he would phone her—*only for business purposes, of course*—but hope had faded midweek. Now it was Friday afternoon and he had casually just dropped in!

'You've run ideas by Nicholas Zentenas?' Her boss sounded as if she was having difficulty with her English. 'Ideas for a new campaign?'

'It was just a few off-the-cuff suggestions.' Cat rose to her feet. 'I told him to come in if he wanted to hear more.'

Victoria's face had turned a strange shade of puce. 'Well… I'm sorry, Cat, but as senior management I will have to handle this.'

'He specifically asked for Cat,' Judy interrupted casually. 'He was most precise on that point. I got the impression that if she wasn't free he would leave.'

The puce shade was turning to purple.

'Don't worry, I'll deal with it, Victoria.' Cat swiftly headed for the door.

'I enjoyed that!' Judy said with a grin as she followed Cat along the corridor towards the lift. 'That woman is getting very irritating.'

Cat couldn't have agreed more, but she was too wound up about the fact that Nicholas was in the building to be able to concentrate on anything else. She brushed a nervous hand over her black pinstripe trousers and then buttoned up the matching waistcoat as she tried to focus her mind on the business aspects of this visit—yet she was aware that her heart was racing with a peculiar emphasis not normally associated with work-related problems.

She wondered if she had time to refresh her lipstick, comb her hair? Maybe not—Nicholas wasn't a man to be kept waiting. The thought had just entered her mind when the lift doors opened and he stepped out.

'Ah, there you are, Cat. I was starting to think you'd got lost.'

He was every bit as commanding as she remembered. Commanding and handsome. A lightweight beige suit fitted the broad-shouldered physique perfectly, hinting at the muscled torso beneath. His dark hair was swept back from his face with a careless indifference that was downright sexy and his dark eyes followed her progress along the corridor with an intensity that made her footsteps falter.

'Sorry to keep you waiting, Mr Zentenas,' Judy called out.

Cat noticed that the indomitable receptionist sounded flustered. It wasn't just her, then—Nicholas probably had this effect on the entire female population. The knowledge helped her to gather herself. She wasn't going to crumble like everyone else.

'Nicholas, this is a pleasant surprise.' Her voice was brisk and businesslike. 'If you had rung, I'd have made an appointment for you so you wouldn't have had to wait.' As she reached his side, she held out her hand.

That was almost her undoing. The firm touch of his skin against hers made her hot and breathless and the amused glint in his eyes told her he knew she wasn't quite as composed as she pretended.

'I found I had a spare half hour and thought I would take a chance that you were free.'

In other words, appointments were for mere mortals; he was above such things and had known she would see him no matter what.

And of course, business-wise, he was right. He was the most impressive and important client to step over her threshold since she had been here.

'Come through to my office.' Cat led him down to the room that had been assigned for her to use when meeting clients. It was effectively the size of a broom cupboard and she left the door open behind them so as to minimise the intimacy of the situation.

'Please sit down.' She waved him towards the leather chair opposite her desk. 'So how has your week been?' She tried to maintain a friendly yet impersonal attitude. 'Have you acquired your new hotel?'

He leaned back in the chair and regarded her laconically. 'The deal is going well.'

'Good.'

Nicholas watched as she manoeuvred herself behind her desk without touching him. The suit looked great on her; the tailored lines of the waistcoat scooped low over her breasts, giving subtle emphasis to her curves. She sat down and reached to open a drawer and he noticed the way her blonde hair spilled silkily over her shoulders and the way her white blouse was unbuttoned, giving a glimpse of a lacy bra and firm rounded flesh. A business outfit had never looked so sexy. He was aware that his mind had moved away from practicalities. It was probably just the thrill of the chase, but Catherine McKenzie was the most attractive woman he had come across in a long time....

'I take it you've had a chance to think about some of the ideas I mentioned last week?' she asked.

He smiled at that.

'Obviously they were just sketchy outlines,' she continued swiftly. Despite the brisk confidence of her tone, there was a sudden vulnerability in her demeanour, her skin flared with heat and the green eyes were shadowed with uncertainty as she slanted a glance towards him.

He knew there was nothing remotely vulnerable about her, but she played the part well, the illusion was tantalizing.

'Anyway, I took the liberty of filling out some of the details for you in case you would be interested.'

He watched as she opened up a file and brought out sheets of paper.

'Now, what I thought was...' She turned the pages around and slid them towards him so that he could see. 'If we started focusing on one hotel and then developed the idea...' She turned over more of the pages. 'We could make a fantastic impact.'

'You have been busy.' Nicholas leaned forward and studied the pages intently.

Busy was an understatement. Cat had worked all last

weekend to finish this for Monday in case he came in. When he hadn't, she had taken it home in the evenings and had honed it some more. It had occupied her every spare minute of the week.

She watched restlessly as he read it and then re-read it. 'Not bad,' he said at last as he sat back.

Not bad! Cat fought down the annoyance that flared at those words. 'I think it will be a massive success,' she said instead with quiet confidence.

'Maybe.' He regarded her for a long moment. Despite his non-committal tone, he was impressed. He just didn't want to tell her that. He intended to make her work a little harder for him first. 'So you recommend concentrating on one hotel—'

'Just to start the ball rolling, because it will give the whole campaign a more personal slant and it will stress the individuality of your hotels.'

Nicholas didn't say anything for a while. Cat could feel the nervous tension knotting inside her but she refrained from pushing her point. She didn't want to sound desperate.

'You might have something with this,' he said finally.

'I know I do.'

'However, selecting the right hotel might be tricky.'

'I don't see why.' Cat picked up the pencil that she had been using earlier and tapped it against the papers. 'You have a lot to choose from. All your hotels are sumptuously upmarket yet unique. But you should select the one with the most character, the most romantic… Yes, that's it. Go for the most romantic.'

He shrugged. 'They say Paris is the most romantic city in the world and I have a superb hotel there overlooking the River Seine, but—'

'A little obvious,' she said quickly.

'Just what I was thinking.'

She smiled at him but it was clear that her mind was racing ahead as she gave the question some thought.

She tapped the pencil against her lips for a second, then ran it softly over the inside of her lower lip.

He knew her mind was firmly on business but Nicholas found the action provocative. She was all brisk professionalism on the outside and wanton sex goddess within. He wanted her…wanted her with even more urgency than before.

'Maybe somewhere closer to home would be better,' she said softly. She remembered the hotel from last weekend with its beautiful restaurant and terraces. 'Isn't there a rumour that Casanova attended a masked ball at your hotel here in London?'

Nicholas laughed at that. 'Yes—there's a commemorative inscription in the ballroom. But—'

'It might be a good hook.'

It wasn't the kind of hook Nicholas was interested in right now. What he wanted was a place far enough away that there would be no distractions…*somewhere he could undress her and have his fill of her at leisure.* 'Actually…you might be on to something there…' he said slowly as an idea occurred to him.

'So does that mean you like the idea enough to go ahead with the campaign?' She fixed him with a direct look, anticipation in the green depths of her eyes.

'No, it means I'm thinking about it.'

She frowned.

'I'll have to look at the hotel with your plans in mind, try and picture your ideas and get back to you.'

'Oh, come on, Nicholas!' She dropped the pencil and the pretence of being laid-back. If he walked out of here now she could be stewing for days about whether he was going to come back or not!

One dark eyebrow lifted wryly as he looked across at her.

'The offer on the table is a good one and you like it—you know you do,' she insisted.

He smiled. Yes, he did like it; it was a definite bonus—but he would like it better if she were on the table alongside. And yes, he knew he had three whole months to work on getting what he wanted. But he was getting a little tired of telling himself to be patient—patience had never been his strong point.

'I tell you what—you come and have dinner with me tonight at the hotel in question and give me your take on exactly how we could use the place for the advert. And then I'll give you a yes or no before the end of the day.'

The offer made a wave of heat sweep through her—heat that had nothing to do with the excitement of business; this was an altogether more dangerous anticipation. And that was why she swiftly turned the invitation down.

'I'm sorry. Unfortunately, I'm busy tonight.' It was a lie; she had nothing at all lined up. But how could she spend an evening with him in romantic surroundings when he made her pulses race like this? Even with a business desk between them it was hard to ignore the attraction she felt for him.

She didn't want to feel like this, she wanted to concentrate on work. She needed this contract!

'Pity.' He stood up. 'This is the only evening that I can spare.'

Cat was suddenly filled with the horrible certainty that she was making a huge mistake! He was going to walk out and she would be left to field her boss's questions without any precise idea on where she stood. And, what was more, if Victoria found out she had turned down a business dinner with Nicholas Zentenas she would be apoplectic!

'Well, maybe I can do some reshuffling,' she said hastily as she also rose to her feet.

'That would be good.' He didn't sound surprised by her

sudden change of heart. Obviously he was used to calling the tune like this. It annoyed her to have to meekly submit but what could she do? It *was* business, she reminded herself firmly. And if he agreed to her ideas she would have to take another look at the hotel anyway, to plan what they could use.

He glanced at his watch. 'What time do you finish here?'

'Another couple of hours.' She frowned. 'Why?'

'I need to make reservations.'

'Well, I could probably be ready for seven-thirty.'

He shook his head. 'You'll have to be ready earlier than that otherwise we won't be eating until after ten.'

'Why so late?'

'It's about a two hour flight to Venice.'

'Venice?' She looked over at him in consternation. 'I thought we'd decided that your hotel here in London would be the best location for the first advert.'

'Who decided that?'

'I thought it was what we agreed!' Her voice rose slightly. She was totally panic-stricken now. She couldn't go to Venice with him! It was bad enough thinking about having dinner with him here in London, let alone flying hundreds of miles away with him!

'I haven't agreed to anything—yet,' he reminded her coolly.

She refused to be intimidated by that. 'Yes, but the hotel here in London would be perfect! It has a great hook because of that masked ball.'

'And the hotel in Venice has a better hook, because Venice is the home of the masked ball.'

She couldn't argue with that.

'So I'll pick you up in about an hour.'

'That's not giving me very much time to get ready! How long is this trip going to take?'

'You don't have to pack anything, if that's what you mean,'

he said laconically. 'I'll have the company jet on standby. You'll be back before midnight. Unless, of course, you would rather stay overnight?'

Their eyes collided across the table.

'No! I've got a busy day lined up tomorrow,' she told him quickly.

He smiled. 'Well, you just need to bring yourself, then.' He tapped the folder on the table. 'Oh, and a copy of this. We mustn't forget why we are there, must we?' he said teasingly.

'There's no chance of that, Nicholas.' She didn't know why she felt the need to say that, but she did.

He seemed to find the words amusing.

For a moment their eyes held and she could feel her heart thudding uncomfortably against her ribs.

She suspected that he knew she was drawn to him against her will. And he was enjoying the fact that he had power over her senses.

Why? Was it just the fact that he was an arrogant male who saw her as some kind of a challenge?

Probably. If she had to put money on it, that was where she would place her bet. She didn't trust him. But then she didn't trust any man, she thought wryly, she knew the deceitful games they could play and Nicholas epitomised everything she most detested in a man—he was arrogant, powerful and interested in only one thing. Money.

But he *was* interested in her business proposal, she reminded herself swiftly. There was no denying that look in his eye when he had leafed through her work.

That was all that mattered. If she secured him as a client, her troubles at Goldstein would be a thing of the past. She would have proved herself without doubt and the contracts would roll in after that. Her student debt would be paid off in no time.

With that in mind she could cope with everything else, including the demons within who lured her into thinking how wonderful it would be to be wrapped in Nicholas's arms.

CHAPTER FIVE

WHEN Cat arrived back at her flat it was after five. Getting away from the office early had not been as easy as she had imagined. For one thing it had taken time to have a few contracts drafted ready for Nicholas to sign. Although she had given her boss a copy of her proposals for the Zentenas campaign and had brought her up to speed with the situation, Victoria had kept her hanging around. She had wanted to go through every detail again, her manner agonizingly slow.

In the end Cat had looked at her watch and had told her bluntly that if she didn't leave now, the deal would probably be in the bin by tomorrow as Nicholas wasn't a man to be kept waiting.

Victoria had shaken her head. 'Well, you'd better go, then,' she had said as she'd closed the files and contracts and slid them back to her. 'Just don't mess this up, Cat. I'll expect a signed contract before you return to the office on Monday.'

The cheek of the woman, Cat thought crossly now as she took the stairs up to her flat two at a time rather than wait for the lift. She had used her own initiative to tempt one of the biggest clients Goldstein had seen in a while and the woman hadn't even said well done!

As she rounded the corner on to her landing she saw her

brother lounging against the wall beside her front door. He brightened as he saw her approach, but Cat's heart sank; she really wasn't in the mood for this right now.

'Hi, sis!' Michael was dark-haired and rangy, not bad-looking in a sullen kind of a way. He always dressed in designer gear; today was no exception, she noted.

Although his tone was friendly, Cat wasn't fooled for one moment; she knew he hadn't come to exchange pleasantries with her.

'Hi, Michael.' Her tone was clipped. 'Sorry I haven't got time to talk. I'm in a rush; I've got a business dinner tonight.'

There was a wounded look in his eyes. 'Cat, I've rung you several times this week and you haven't returned one of my calls. When will you have time to talk to me?'

'Maybe after my twenty-first birthday.' She gave him a pointed look. 'When we can drop the subject of the inheritance money.'

'I can't believe you are being so unreasonable!' His good looks screwed into a frown. 'This is important. I need that money, Cat! Business is slow. I'm really stretched.'

Michael always told her that business was slow. But he was living in an apartment at Canary Wharf and she guessed if she glanced out of the window she would see his red sports car parked by the kerb. She wasn't sure if her brother was just living beyond his means...or lying to her completely. Only one thing was sure—no matter how much money he had, it was never enough.

'I'm sorry to hear that,' she said, getting her front door key out. 'But I just haven't got time for this.'

'So you're not going to do anything about claiming our inheritance?' he asked abruptly as she turned away.

He always referred to the money as *our* inheritance...and

Cat never argued the point. 'If you mean am I planning my wedding …then the answer is no, Michael, I am not.'

'For goodness' sake, Cat,' he grated. 'You could do with some of that money yourself! Your life isn't that great; you are living in a shoebox, working all hours and you don't make great money.'

'I'm doing all right,' she said curtly. 'And I'm happy.'

'You are used to better things, Cat. You were brought up in luxury.'

'I'm sorry, Michael, but I'm not marrying just to get that money.'

He raked a hand through his hair. 'Dad and I have been talking—'

'Good for you.' Cat put the key into the lock and opened the door. She didn't want to hear any more. 'Please go, Michael.'

'Just give me one minute.' Michael reached into his pocket, took something out and shoved it towards her.

'What's this?' Startled, Cat took the piece of paper and, glancing down, found she was looking at a photograph of a dark-haired man in his twenties.

'He's called Peter and he's a friend of mine. I've told him about our problem and he's willing to meet you at the register office and tie the knot… You never need to see him again.'

Cat felt a wave of fury. 'It never ceases to amaze me how low you will stoop.' She tried to push the photograph back towards him but he wouldn't take it.

'Look, I'm being upfront with you this time—I know I shouldn't have deceived you and set you up with Ryan. And this is just a means to an end,' he insisted. 'I've had a word with a lawyer friend and we can draw up a prenuptial agreement so that the money is secured. And Peter would be very happy with the arrangement. So you see everyone will win from this situation.'

'You can forget it, Michael. I'm not doing it!' she said flatly.

Michael stared at her calmly. 'That money should never have been left to you, Cat. By rights it belongs to Dad. You know that.'

'I'm not responsible for the way the will was left!' Cat glared at him. 'Is Dad happy with this? Does he really want me to marry a total stranger?'

'He thinks it's a great idea!'

A sharp stab of pain twisted inside her. Hurriedly she turned away and, before her brother could stop her, she went into her flat and slammed the door.

'Just think about it!' Michael's voice was muffled from outside.

She squeezed her eyes tightly closed; it didn't come as any real surprise that her father cared so little about her. They hadn't been close in a long time and deep down she had known something like this would be suggested. But it still hurt because he was her father and because she remembered a time before her mother had died when she had idolised him. Pulling herself together, she threw the photograph to one side.

She had discovered a long time ago that her idol had feet of clay. Feeling sad didn't solve anything; she just had to get on with her life. And that meant throwing herself into work and forgetting about relationships.

Nicholas pulled up outside Cat's flat at a little after six. He felt a gleam of satisfaction at the way things were playing out; it was reminiscent of the way he felt when he was about to close a major business deal. In fact, if anything the thrust of adrenalin was perhaps greater. The scent of revenge was close and sweetly exhilarating.

He stepped out of the limousine into the warmth of the evening and strolled towards the entrance of the old Victorian building. Cat lived in a decent area; the road was tree-lined and had an air of prosperity about it. But Nicholas knew it was a million miles away from how she had lived when she was growing up.

He wondered not for the first time what she was planning to do to get her inheritance. She was a beautiful woman and could have bagged herself a husband without too much of a problem but, according to his sources, she had no boyfriend. Apparently there had been someone in her life last year but it hadn't worked out—now she just had casual dates every now and then. She seemed to be content playing the field with her friends, living her life like any normal twenty-year-old.

Maybe she was wary of marriage as a partner could walk away with a chunk of the inheritance. She might have decided to keep her options open; the money would be hers in nine years anyhow, with or without marriage. But of course waiting wouldn't please her father or brother. They, no doubt, had plans and schemes for that money.

As Cat had gone along with their schemes in the past, maybe she was content to do so again. In that case they would be organizing some kind of arranged marriage—some deal that would prevent a new husband having a legal claim on what was theirs. The thought made a twist of distaste stir inside him.

Whatever they were planning, they were going to be very disappointed. He smiled to himself as he stepped out of the lift and rang her doorbell. He would really like to see the look on their faces the morning they woke up and realized that someone had got to the pot of gold first.

The door swung open. Cat was wearing a plain black dress that hugged her slender figure. She looked businesslike, but so sexy and breathtakingly beautiful that he almost forgot why he was here.

'Hello, I'm nearly ready.' She stepped back from the door, her manner brisk. 'Come in for a moment.'

Nicholas wrenched his eyes away from her as he stepped inside and focused his attention on the surroundings.

The flat wasn't at all what he had been expecting. He had assumed because it was in an old Victorian building that the rooms would be huge, but the place was small. She had decorated with style, however; it had a homely, welcoming feel. Bright canvases adorned the white walls and the old sofas were draped with throws and scatter cushions in a rich gold and tangerine. One alcove was filled with books and there were fresh flowers in a crystal vase on the mantelpiece.

'Sorry to keep you waiting,' she said coolly.

His glance moved back to her. She was perched on the arm of the sofa, slipping on a pair of high-heeled court shoes.

She had lovely legs, he noticed. They were very long and very shapely. In fact everything about her was enticing. His eyes travelled upwards over the silk stockings and the knee-length dress, noting that she wore no jewellery to adorn the square neckline. Her hair was secured in a casual twist with an amber comb. The style drew attention to the long length of her neck

Cat looked over at him. She was well aware of his scrutiny and she was trying very hard not to let it unnerve her. 'I had…' As their eyes connected she almost forgot what she was saying. There was something almost primal in the way he was looking at her, as if he were touching her, possessing her with his gaze. It made her senses flood with wild heat and she hated that! With difficulty she maintained her poise. 'I had difficulty getting away from the office. It's been a very busy day.'

'It will be a busy day on the roads too; Friday always is.' He glanced at his watch. 'The road to the airport will be jammed if we don't leave soon.'

His tone was businesslike, totally at odds with the way he had just looked at her. She didn't know if that made her feel better or not—she couldn't work out the undercurrent between them at all. 'I just need my passport. Won't be a second.'

It was a relief to escape into the bedroom and, although her passport was sitting on top of her dressing table, she didn't immediately pick it up; instead, she took a few moments to compose herself.

This feeling of desire that attacked her senses every time she looked at him was going to have to stop. For one thing, she couldn't allow anything to mess up the opportunity of this business contract—that was all that mattered. For another Nicholas Zentenas had danger written all over him.

If she lowered her defences around him he would take what he wanted and then walk away to get on with the business of making money. She would mean less than nothing, and she wasn't going to allow any man to treat her like that. Snatching up her passport, she returned to the lounge.

She was taken aback to find him studying the photograph that she had flung down on the sofa earlier. 'Who's this?' he asked casually.

'Nobody.' Cat flinched as he turned it over. She knew the words *Looking forward to meeting you* were scrawled on the back, along with a telephone number. 'It's just some friend of my brother,' she found herself adding hurriedly.

'Trying to fix you up on a date, is he?'

The sardonic observation hit a nerve. 'How do you know I'm not already seeing someone?'

'As you attended a wedding party on your own last week, I assume you are unattached. Am I wrong?'

She would have liked to lie but somehow she just couldn't so she found herself shaking her head.

The ring of his mobile phone halted the conversation and Cat was extremely glad of the interruption. How dared he ask about that photograph and her social life? It was none of his business.

As he spoke on the phone Nicholas put the photograph down on the table and she took her chance and went across to pick it up and toss it out of sight into a drawer. She didn't want to talk about it; she didn't even want to think about it or Michael or her father, because when she did it felt as if someone had taken a sledgehammer straight to her heart.

Nicholas watched her through narrowed eyes.

'That was our pilot,' he told her as he hung up. 'Our departure is scheduled for less than an hour.'

'Well, I'm ready.' She slammed the drawer closed with her hip.

There was something determined about the action. 'Got a drawer full of potential beaus in there, have you?'

'Well, you know what brothers are like. They only want the best for their sisters.' She matched his flippant tone but inside the lie hurt. She wished so much that was true.

Nicholas watched as she picked up her briefcase and her bag. She was one cool customer, he thought. Obviously his suspicions were correct and once more she was planning to go along with her family's shady ideas. Daddy had probably sewn up some poor guy and got him to agree to the union for a pittance. He felt a twist of pure distaste. The words *as thick as thieves* sprang to mind.

Yet there was something about the way she held herself, the proud tilt of her head, the sparkle of her green eyes, that made another emotion flood through him—determination. No matter how far Carter or Michael McKenzie were prepared to go he was prepared to go, further. He was the one who would claim Cat and the inheritance.

Nicholas's limousine waited at the kerb and a chauffeur jumped out and opened the doors for them.

It was luxuriously fitted out inside and extremely comfortable. If it hadn't been for the situation, Cat might have enjoyed the drive. But she was intensely aware of Nicholas in every way—his cologne, the light touch of his arm against hers, even the silence seemed loaded with tension.

She kept her gaze averted from him and searched for something to say—something that would break this feeling.

Clearing her throat, she made an attempt at business. 'Have you thought any more about what we discussed this afternoon?'

He glanced over at her. 'All in good time, Cat.'

He was infuriating, she thought. 'Don't forget that you did promise to give me an answer before the end of the evening,' she felt compelled to remind him. She didn't want him stringing her along. Men were good at that and she wasn't going to be walked over.

'Oh, I haven't forgotten anything,' Nicholas assured her. 'But, until we actually get to the hotel, there is little new of value that we can discuss—businesswise, that is.'

Their eyes met.

'So I suggest that we relax,' he continued smoothly. 'The flight will take about two hours so we may as well use the time to relax, get to know each other a little better...hmm?'

His words and the way he was looking at her held a provocative power that made her temperature sizzle.

With difficulty she tried to dismiss the feeling. 'Actually, there is a lot we didn't cover this afternoon,' she said firmly. 'I thought we could go over some of the ideas for the follow-up adverts.'

'I think we need to walk before we can run,' he contradicted silkily.

He really was maddening but she couldn't think of a suitable reply because the way he looked at her made all her thoughts run riot. She fell silent and for a moment their eyes held.

Hurriedly she glanced away from him and out of the

window. They were on an airfield now and she could see a private jet ready and waiting with the steps down.

It wasn't too late to turn tail and run, a little voice told her insistently.

And how would that look in the office on Monday morning? she asked herself sternly. She was being ridiculous.

They pulled to a standstill within a few feet of the aircraft and their driver came around to open the passenger doors for them. The noise from the aircraft filled her eardrums as they stepped out into the warmth of the sunlight.

'Good evening, Mr Zentenas.' The man waiting for them had to practically shout to make himself heard. 'Everything is ready for you, sir, exactly as stipulated.'

What had Nicholas stipulated? Cat wondered. But there was no time for further conversation; Nicholas waved her to go ahead of him up the steps into the aeroplane.

She was amazed when she stepped inside to find that it was unlike any other aircraft she had ever travelled in. Deep leather seats faced each other across a desk. There was a state-of-the-art office to one side, and through a door at the back she could see a double bed.

Had Nicholas been thinking about that bed when he had suggested using the flight time to get to know each other? The thought filtered through her and with it a deep burning swirl of pure desire.

Fiercely she tried to maintain a sense of perspective. Yes, Nicholas probably wouldn't mind amusing himself with her to pass a few spare hours, but did she really want to be used as some millionaire's plaything for a few fleeting hours of short-lived pleasure? This was an important business trip. She wanted him to treat her seriously—not as some sex kitten.

Nicholas joined her in the cabin and immediately the door

of the plane was closed behind him with a heavy clunk that almost matched the slam of her heart.

'Everything OK?' He smiled over at her.

'Yes, thank you.' She put her briefcase in an overhead compartment and then selected a seat so that her back was towards the bedroom. She really didn't want to be reminded of that for the entire journey.

Nicholas took off his suit jacket and put it away in another compartment. The white shirt he wore was open at the neck; she noticed the wide muscular width of his shoulders, the lithe hips, the very taut line of his buttocks—before quickly looking away again.

He took his place in the seat opposite and a few moments later the engine noise increased and the safety belt sign was illuminated.

'The pilot doesn't believe in hanging around,' she said lightly, trying to stem the rising feelings of apprehension.

'We've got a clearance slot from air traffic control for take-off and if we don't take it immediately we could be hanging around on the tarmac for another hour.'

Cat looked out of the porthole as the plane taxied on to the runway, then stopped. There were a few moments while they just sat and waited. Her eyes met Nicholas's and the feeling of tension inside her escalated wildly.

'Do you like flying?' he asked nonchalantly.

'I don't dislike it.' The feelings inside her were nothing to do with flying and everything to do with him. 'It gets you places quickly… It's a means to an end, isn't it?'

He smiled at that. 'It is indeed.'

Was it her imagination or was his reply loaded with some other meaning?

The engine noise suddenly whooshed into powerful life as the jet thundered down the runway at a speed that made Cat's stomach feel as if it had been left behind. Outside the window Cat could see that London was already looking like toy-town, the grid pattern of the roads and the parks getting smaller as they climbed higher. Then they straightened out and a few moments later the seat belt sign went out.

Nicholas unfastened his belt and stood up. 'Would you like a drink?' He moved towards a fridge at the far side of the cabin and looked around at her enquiringly.

'Just water, please,' she said briskly. 'I want to keep a clear head.'

He smiled at that.

'Have I said something amusing?'

'No. I just wondered if you ever did anything other than keep a clear head and think about business.'

She tried to ignore the remark, but it rankled. 'That's rich, coming from you!'

'How's that?'

'Well, you must never think of anything other than making money! How else would you achieve all this?' She spread her hands, indicating the luxurious aircraft.

'I work hard when necessary and I'm focused. But I also play hard.'

'I'll bet.' Cat couldn't resist the retort. 'Money mogul by day and playboy by night.'

Nicholas laughed at that.

He had a nice laugh, she thought. It was warm and provocative and infinitely sexy. Their eyes met as he passed her the glass of water.

'Is that how you see me?'

She shrugged and looked away from him, feeling most uncomfortable now. What on earth had possessed her to say such a thing? 'How you live your life is none of my business.'

'No, it's not,' he agreed smoothly. 'But you've obviously

made some sweeping assessments anyway. I noticed this about you when we first met.' He sat down again in the seat opposite.

'Noticed what, exactly?'

'I suppose you would call it an inbuilt wariness.' He took a sip of his drink and watched her skin tinge with colour.

'I don't know what you mean,' she said stiffly.

'No?' The amusement was still there in the darkness of his eyes. 'My mistake, then.'

It rankled that she amused him. 'Well, you are obviously a playboy,' she muttered in annoyance. 'You are—what—thirty and unmarried?'

'Thirty-three and divorced,' he cut across her wryly.

She was surprised by the disclosure. She hadn't realized he was divorced.

'You see, you don't know me at all. And before you hazard a guess, it was my wife who was—now, how is it you English put it?—playing away.'

She frowned; he was right that she had made a lot of assumptions about him.

'On the first night we met you accused me of wanting to cheat on my partner,' he reminded her with a grin. 'You assumed, in fact, that it was a mode of behaviour that I would regularly put into practice.'

'I did apologise for saying that.' She shifted uncomfortably.

'Do you know what I think?' He looked over at her with a bold light in his dark eyes. 'I think you're so attracted to me that you have to keep telling yourself these things so that you can fight the feelings.'

The fact that he wasn't far wide of the mark was very disconcerting. 'And do you know what I think?' she retorted quickly. 'I think that you are one of the most arrogant men I have ever met.'

'There you go again...another excuse.' His eyes glinted

mockingly. 'You've got a better defence system than London has with the Thames Barrier.'

'And you've got an even bigger ego.'

He laughed and relaxed back in his chair. 'You know, I enjoy our little sparring sessions; they are like an exhilarating form of foreplay…don't you think?'

'No, I don't.' She glared at him.

'If the real thing is anything as fiery, I think we would need flame-proof bedding,' he continued.

'Why don't you just drink your whisky and we'll get down to business?' she said. He really was going too far with this.

'Actually, I'm drinking iced tea.' He smiled at her. 'And I've never been propositioned quite so bluntly before.'

'You know exactly what I mean.'

He laughed. It was strange, but he did enjoy sparring with her. Most people deferred to him. Women especially tended to submit eagerly and immediately to his ideas and needs. But Cat's eyes glinted and blazed with feeling. She was like a wild kitten that needed taming—he just needed to keep in mind that she may look beautiful but she was a kitten hiding extremely treacherous claws.

'Shall we forget this nonsensical conversation and look at the plans I have drawn up for the campaign?' she continued crisply. Her green eyes held with his but beneath the cool, competent veneer there was a flame that excited him beyond reason.

Oh, yes, he was very much looking forward to breaking her will until she was purring and submissive to his every desire.

He smiled and pretended to relent. 'Go ahead, take your papers out.' But in truth he had no intention of looking at her business plans just yet. They could wait until later.

Nicholas watched as she unfastened her seat belt and stood up. He was treated to a pleasurable view of her figure as she stretched to open the overhead compartment.

Desire escalated inside him and he allowed her to struggle with the catch for a few moments more before offering assistance. He knew full well that she couldn't get into the compartment because he'd locked it with a flick of a button just before take off.

'Need some help?' he asked laconically.

'Yes—it seems to be stuck.' As she stepped back from it, he surreptitiously pressed the button on the arm of his chair releasing the lock and then stood up to help.

She watched with a sense of frustration as Nicholas opened the compartment with ease and took out her briefcase. He put it down on the desk beside them but didn't immediately return to his seat.

'Thanks.'

'You're welcome.' He returned some files that had been sitting in a rack by the door into the locker. 'I'll just tidy these away.'

The confines of the aisle meant she couldn't get back to her seat without moving nearer to him and, as she was too close for comfort as it was, she stood and waited.

'You've got a great office in here,' she remarked, trying to take her mind off the way his muscles flexed under the fine silk material of his shirt.

'Yes it comes in useful when I'm on business trips. Means I can utilise my time efficiently—'

Cat's gaze moved towards the sliding door through to the bedroom. He caught the glance and smiled. 'And I like my creature comforts.'

'So I noticed—' Her words were abruptly halted as the plane hit some turbulence and gave an unexpectedly violent judder.

'Are you all right?' He reached and caught hold of her arm and then the plane lurched again and she lost her balance completely and found herself slammed against his chest. His arm went around her, steadying her, holding her close.

The shock of the contact was immense; it flooded through her system, disorientating her like a shot of some mind-altering drug. And in that second wrapped in his arms she was achingly aware that this was a place she wanted to be. Here loneliness was relegated to the furthest corners of her heart, chased away by the hard, powerful body crushed against hers.

'Cat?'

She was vaguely aware that the plane had stopped shuddering and that he was waiting for her to answer him.

With difficulty she lifted her head from his chest and looked up at him. Something happened as their eyes met, something that sent wild spirals of heat pulsating through her.

'Sorry…I lost my balance.'

'You don't need to apologise,' he said with a smile.

Danger signals escalated and she tried to make herself move away from him but her limbs wouldn't cooperate.

His gaze moved towards the sensual curve of her lips and her heart skipped violently against her chest.

'So…what are we going to do about this?' he asked softly.

'Do about what?' Her voice was no more than a husky whisper.

'This…' He reached out a hand to stroke it down along the long line of her neck. The caress made the heat of sexual need increase; she could feel it curling inside her now as if it were a living entity.

She swallowed hard, terrified by the feeling and desperate to dismiss it.

'I don't know what you mean.'

He laughed; it was a low, very sensual growl of a laugh that made her tingle. 'I think you do.'

There was a purposeful gleam in the darkness of his eyes that made her pulses race. Then suddenly he lowered his head towards hers and fear was replaced by a wild excitement. For a moment it didn't matter that she was probably playing with fire. All that mattered was that he was going to kiss her.

As his lips captured hers the world seemed to tip and spin on its axis and this time it had nothing to do with the turbulence outside the aircraft. This time the turbulence was in her heart and in her senses, pounding through her with a relentless searing force.

Cat felt so light-headed that she had to reach up and put her hands on his shoulders to steady herself. And at the touch of her hands his kiss changed from gently persuasive to powerfully fervent, crushing against hers with an almost ruthless intensity.

She kissed him back with equal passion, meeting his demands with a hunger she had never realized lay within her.

In that moment Cat wanted him with every thread of her soul. Desire pumped through her as if someone had broken open a door to a reservoir of need...a reservoir that was so secret that even she hadn't known of its existence until this very moment.

Nicholas was the one to pull back from her, leaving her shaky and bewildered by what had happened.

'That was some kiss,' he murmured.

'Was it?' She tried very hard to sound casually indifferent but, to her distress, her voice was breathless and shaken. She was furious with herself for responding to him like that. 'I didn't notice anything...special...'

Although she tilted her chin defiantly, Nicholas could see a chink in her armour, a receptive light in her eyes.

He smiled. 'A sexual heat exists between us, Catherine. We've both known about it very forcefully since the first moment our eyes met.'

Even the way he spoke her name sounded dangerously provocative. She started to shake her head, but his hands were around her waist now, pulling her back into his arms.

'This is inevitable,' he murmured, 'because the truth is that you want me as much as I want you; I can see that in your eyes, taste it on your lips.'

'It was just a kiss, a reckless spur of the moment kind of wildness…'

She was desperate to justify her response, to herself as much as to him.

'It was more than that.' As he spoke his hands moved upwards, boldly stroking over the firm curves of her breast. He found her nipples through the soft material of her dress and brushed his thumbs over them in a rough caress. It was a blatant demonstration of the power he wielded over her senses because, to her shame, they hardened even more beneath his touch until they were throbbing with need.

Cat closed her eyes and desperately tried to fight against the erotic sensation that flooded through her, but her body was crying out for more. She wanted him so badly, wanted him to tear away her dress and her underwear and just assuage this unbearable aching need.

'You do want me, Catherine.'

The arrogant words should have made her pull away but she couldn't; she was so aroused by the way he was touching her that she was powerless to fight against it.

CHAPTER SIX

His lips trailed up along the sides of her neck in a heated blaze before capturing her mouth again. And at the same time she felt his hands moving over her possessively, pulling up her dress, finding the lace tops of her stockings and then stroking higher over her naked flesh to the flimsy lace briefs. Cat found herself pressed back against the wall that led through to the connecting room, her arms wound around his shoulders, her fingers raking through the dark thickness of his hair.

'Tell me you want me,' he demanded and, as he spoke, his hand moved to pull at her flimsy underwear, tearing the briefs so that they fell easily away to leave him unconstrained access. When his fingers found the warm wet centre of her she gasped in ecstasy and shock.

In the past she had always been coolly in control of her desires, had always been able to pull away without difficulty. The feelings inside her now were totally different. She was shocked that Nicholas could touch her in a way that made her lose her mind to pleasure, made her writhe instinctively against him.

'Tell me,' he demanded again, his voice fiercely insistent.

'You know I do.' She whispered the words incoherently and saw a smile of satisfaction curve the sensual line of his lips.

His fingers continued to tease her softly while his other hand unfastened the hook at the back of her dress and, with a practised ease, pulled it down to reveal the black lace of her bra and the creamy swell of her breasts.

'You are very beautiful, Catherine...provocatively bewitching and ready for me, is that not so?' He switched to speaking in Greek almost without realizing it. Holding on to his control by a thread, all he wanted now was to plunge himself into her soft warmth, to take her here and now against the wall and watch as she shuddered and convulsed against him. The mere thought almost made him burst with crazy feverish anticipation but he forced himself to control it...forced his mind to think instead of the revenge he wanted—the control he needed.

She wanted him, she would do anything now for release, and he could taste her need as his mouth covered hers, his tongue moving against hers. One hand moved to push away the restraint of her bra and his mouth travelled downwards so that he could take one rosy erect nipple into his mouth.

Her body was gorgeous, her curves lusciously full. His tongue licked against her, noting how her breasts tilted upwards in response to him, inviting his mouth.

She arched her back in ecstasy and drew in her breath in a shuddering sigh as he took her inside the warmth of his mouth, nuzzling her, softly sucking one moment and then taunting her with the tip of his tongue the next.

'Nicholas...please...please.' Cat didn't know what she was saying any more; she was almost delirious with need. In fact, if someone had asked her name right now she wouldn't have known it.

'Please what?' he mocked her softly, his hand moving to cup her pert derrière and press her against him. 'Is it this that you want...?'

She could feel his arousal straining against the material of his suit, large and tauntingly hidden from reach.

'Yes...' As she gave the answer she felt her heart miss a beat almost as violently as the way the aircraft had shuddered earlier. 'Yes, Nicholas, I want you... now.' She closed her eyes and capitulated to the weakness that screamed insistently inside her. Maybe if she sated this desire now she would be able to forget about it and he would no longer wield this power over her senses? She urgently wanted to be back in control—almost as much as she wanted him.

When he made no move to comply with her words—just continued to hold her back against the wall—her eyes flicked open and met his.

The shimmering green eyes were hauntingly beautiful. She was his for the taking. His hand toyed with the triangle of hair between her legs, feeling her wetness and enjoying the low moan that escaped from her throat.

'Nicholas...? Please...'

The whispered plea echoed inside him. He had her completely within his power. Right now she would do anything for him. He wanted to take her, absorb himself completely into her womanly core. But he was aware that, once he sated her, his power would momentarily diminish.

Nicholas leaned closer and kissed the side of her neck and, breathing in her perfume, he forced himself to focus. This wasn't simply about sex, he reminded himself forcefully. If his plan for revenge was to succeed, he needed to draw her closer than that and, to keep the reins of control, he needed to keep her hungry. Therefore pulling back now would be the right decision; it would facilitate his plans for the rest of the evening and make it much easier to manipulate his way under her defence mechanism.

'Maybe now isn't the right moment for this.' It took every

shred of willpower that he possessed to draw away and coolly say those words.

'What do you mean?' Her voice trembled slightly and he saw the incomprehension in her beautiful eyes.

'I mean that in about half an hour we will be landing.' His gaze raked over the breasts that were still swollen with arousal from the warmth of his mouth and his erection throbbed viciously.

Why the hell hadn't he just taken her and alleviated his desire here and now? The question held a kick like an angry mule.

With determination he shut the thought out and forced himself to concentrate. 'A quick release isn't going to put out this fire.'

She shot him a hurt look.

'That was blunt.' He held up his hands. 'I'm sorry.'

'Well, I'm not!' She was hurriedly reaching to cover her nakedness from him now, pulling up her bra and her dress with hands that were shaking. 'I'm glad you've put it in context—it's helped bring me to my senses. I don't know what I was thinking.'

For some reason the huskiness of her tone disconcerted him. 'Catherine.' He reached and caught hold of her, stilling her hands.

There was a mutinous expression in her eyes as she looked up at him but behind that fierce gleam there was something else—a rawness that caught him completely off guard.

Cat looked away from him, scared in case he saw how hurt she was. He was the first man she had ever wanted to give herself to and he had rejected her. But it wasn't just the rejection that hurt—it was the way he had spoken to her as if she were…less than nothing. And yet his caresses had been so tenderly provocative, his kisses had tasted as if they meant something. How could she have been so stupid as to imagine he might actually have feelings for her?

'What I meant to say in a very clumsy way was that the

passion between us is so intense that it would be almost a sin not to savour it at leisure.'

She tried to close her emotions, shut out the power his gently coaxing tone had over her senses. 'The only sin would be if I allowed you to touch me again!'

Nicholas smiled to himself—ah, now, this emotion was one he understood. 'I've hurt your pride.'

'You have not!' She glared at him. 'I just can't believe that I allowed this to go as far as it did. We are supposed to be discussing business plans, not…not having a…a quick…' She couldn't bring herself to refer to it the way he had. 'Anyway, you know what I mean.'

He smiled. 'Yes, I know what you mean. And we will discuss our business over dinner and then I will take you to bed.'

'You will not!'

He laughed. 'But it is inevitable, Catherine.' As he spoke, he straightened her dress, allowing his hand to run lightly over the top of her breast, feeling her instant response to him. 'You see? We'll stay overnight at the hotel.' His voice was cool. It wasn't a request—it was a demand.

Before she could say anything else, he leaned closer and captured her lips in a slow-burning, sensual kiss that made her whole body turn over with longing—the feeling blew her mind. She still wanted him; in fact, if anything, the hunger she felt inside was sharpened.

She couldn't look at him as he pulled away; all her life she'd had no problem in exercising restraint and now, when she needed it most, the ability seemed to have completely vanished.

The aircraft gave a jolt as it hit some more turbulence.

'We'll be landing soon. We should return to our seats,' Nicholas said coolly. He watched as she ran a smoothing hand down over her dress and then reached to pick up the flimsy lacy briefs that were on the floor.

They were ripped and beyond use and, with embarrassment, she was forced to step out of them.

Nicholas watched as she reached to pick them up. 'You won't need those, anyway.' He calmly took them from her and tossed them in the wastepaper bin beside the desk. 'I don't want you to wear underwear tonight. I want to know I can touch you—whenever I might please.'

'You really are the most arrogant and...' she searched desperately for adjectives to describe him '...egotistical man I have ever met!'

He laughed. 'But you still want me.' The gleam of self-assurance in his tone made her bite down on her lip so hard that she could taste blood.

'No, I don't! I don't want you to touch me ever again!'

He touched her face lightly and even the soft caress brought forcibly home the fact that she was lying. He was right—she did still want him. Flinching away from him, she returned to her seat, aware that Nicholas was calmly returning her briefcase into the locker.

A limousine met them at the airport. Cat sat as far away as possible from Nicholas as it swept them away down a narrow country road. She stared out at the dark landscape and tried to get the turmoil inside her under some control. Winning the account for Goldstein was what mattered, she told herself furiously. Nothing should be allowed to interfere with that. What had happened—or nearly happened—between them on the journey here meant nothing.

She bit down on her lip and tried not to think about how she had felt when she was in his arms, how she had begged him to make love to her. What worried her most was that bizarre sense of how right it had felt to be held by him—and the feeling of hurt when he had pulled away so cavalierly. Cat had always sworn that a man would never use her the way her father had used her mother.

Early on in her teenage years she remembered that she had questioned her father about his affair with Julia. Had asked him bluntly if her mother had known about it.

'Of course she did.' He had shrugged. 'She put up with it because she wanted to—because she wanted me.'

The words had stayed with her. Her mother's situation was a salutary lesson on how important it was to stay in control, never let your guard down.

'Cat?' Nicholas's voice brought her out of her reverie and she realized the car had pulled to a halt down by the edge of a ferry terminal. 'We have to take a boat from here.'

'Fine.' Gathering her briefcase up, she stepped out into the warmth of the evening air.

Nicholas watched as she walked ahead of him down on to a wooden jetty. She seemed coolly composed and he knew she was making a determined effort to erect her barriers and retreat from him. He had to admit he was impressed by how quickly she had been able to do that. In all honesty he still felt as if he needed to take a very cold shower.

He couldn't remember the last time he had wanted a woman so desperately and it amazed him that he could feel this level of attraction for a woman who was a McKenzie— cunning and fraudulent.

They stood in silence on the pontoon. It was a clear night and a full moon shimmered down over the water, casting it with a silvery glow. Nicholas noticed how it also held Cat as if in a spotlight, highlighting the luscious curves of her figure and turning her hair to the colour of spun gold, her skin to porcelain. As if sensing his gaze she glanced over at him, her eyes jewel-bright, seeming too large, too intense for the delicate face. He sensed anger first in the blaze of her look—but then something else—a poignancy that hit him like a blazing arrow. She didn't look like someone who was cunning and fraudulent; she looked—pure—like a girl afraid to trust, afraid of her emotions.

Then, with a sweep of long dark eyelashes, the look was gone. A trick of the light, he told himself sharply. But the protective feelings the illusion had roused were slow to recede and that made him angry with himself. He couldn't allow himself to get sidetracked and deceived by her beauty and by the fact that he wanted her. What she looked like on the outside and who she really was were two entirely different things.

She put up barriers to assert a rigid control over her emotions. He couldn't quite work out why she did that or what drove her. Maybe just a natural need to be focused on business—maybe just a determination to be as tough and ruthless as the rest of her family. Yes, probably the latter.

Nicholas had learnt a thing or two about women since his divorce. He had learnt that they could be naturally duplicitous; they could draw you in with a soft smile and a delicate femininity that hid a tough calculating mind.

He remembered the look on Cat's face earlier as she had tossed the photograph of the man her father had lined up for her into the drawer. It had been a look of resolve. His first assessment of her had been correct. Catherine McKenzie was nothing but a siren—and she certainly didn't need anyone's protection.

'Here's our water taxi now,' he said briskly as the distant chug of a boat cut the silence.

Considering they were at the gateway to a large city, the place was strangely deserted, the only sound the taxi as it pulled in beside them, then, as it cut its engine, just the swish of the sea against the platform.

Cat felt as if she had reached more than a gateway to a

city—she felt as if she had reached a threshold and, once she stepped over it, there would be no going back. Hastily she told herself that she was being fanciful. She would conduct herself in a businesslike manner, get Nicholas to agree to the ad campaign and then she would insist he take her back to the airport and home. Despite the firm assurances, she could feel her heart thumping against her chest in slow painful beats.

Nicholas jumped down into the boat and then held a hand out to assist her. She pointedly ignored it and stepped down unaided. The boat rocked slightly but she managed to keep her balance and her dignity and move past him to sit down at the back. A few moments later he sat beside her. He was too close for comfort; she could feel the warmth of his thigh pressed against her, smell the provocative scent of his cologne. She wanted to move away but there was nowhere to go.

The engine flared into life and the boat backed out into the dark silky waters before turning and skipping across the waves with speed. The night air was hot against her skin, the spray from the boat misting in the air, white against the stark darkness. Then the boat rounded a corner and she could see the city shimmering in golden light. The domes of the cathedrals and churches, the bridges and the dark shapes of the gondolas moored alongside were like something from a film set. It looked so beautiful that she drew in her breath in pleasure.

'First time in Venice?' Nicholas's voice close against her ear made her senses quiver in response.

She nodded, aware that if she turned her head a fraction towards him their lips would meet. Instantly the feeling of need that had overwhelmed her earlier started to surface again.

'Tomorrow, if we can get out of bed, I will take you out and show you the sights if you'd like.'

The self-assured words seared against her consciousness. 'Tomorrow I will be back in London,' she stated firmly.

He laughed but said nothing. For the time being he was content to allow her to pull her barriers up. For the next hour or two he wanted to concentrate on the ad campaign. Business was important and her ideas merited a deep consideration. But once work was out of the way, he would bring her back to where he wanted her. He was confident after the way he had left things earlier that he wouldn't have too much difficulty with that. Once he held her in his arms again she would realize the futility of pretending and she would be his—totally his to take again and again as he pleased.

After that her defences would be trampled to dust, paving the way for his ultimate goal—revenge.

CHAPTER SEVEN

THE Hotel Zentenas was a magnificently restored palace that had been designed in the late fourteenth century to meet the requirements of Europe's travelling nobility. Its impressive exterior was lit up by golden lights that reflected softly over a small terrace at one side with ornamental box hedges and yew trees and shimmered over the waters of the canal.

The water taxi left them directly at the private pontoon leading up to the front door. And this time as Cat left the vessel she was forced to take Nicholas's hand as the boat bobbed unsteadily beneath her and the water swished against the building.

'Are you OK?' he asked solicitously, keeping hold of her as she found her balance.

'Yes, thank you.' She pulled away from the warmth of his grasp and tried to ignore the heat that even the most casual of contact seemed to stir up inside her. Instead she turned her attention to the hotel.

The heavy front door lay open and as they stepped inside Cat was completely overawed by the majesty of her surroundings. Enormous Murano glass chandeliers lit the medieval entrance hall, sparkling over Persian rugs and marble floors. Candlelight flickered in the deep recesses by the mullioned windows; antique gilded furniture and sumptuously comfortable sofas were positioned there for privacy and relaxation. And further back at one side there was a reception desk in polished rosewood, at the other an imposing staircase.

It was a lesson on how a place could be luxuriously refurbished without losing its authenticity and character. And Cat was completely enchanted by it.

'I thought your hotel in London was fabulous, but this is something really special,' she said softly.

'Yes, I have to admit this place is a particular favourite of mine,' Nicholas said with a smile. 'It has a unique character.'

Before Cat had time to answer, the hotel manager hurried over to welcome them.

'Nicholas, it is good to see you again,' he said as they shook hands.

'You too, Antonio,' Nicholas smiled and then smoothly introduced him to Cat.

Antonio Belgravi was a tall handsome Italian in his late thirties. His dark sensual eyes flared with undisguised interest as they fell on her. 'Ms McKenzie, it is indeed a pleasure to meet you,' he said as he took her hand and, to Cat's surprise raised it to his lips.

'Call me Cat, please, everyone does.' She tried to sound nonchalant but, in honesty, she was a little embarrassed by the warmth of his welcome.

Nicholas watched as a faint tinge of colour lit the pallor of her skin and felt a twist of impatience. 'Shall we get on?' he said abruptly. 'We have rather a lot of business to get through and then we will dine, Antonio. You did make the necessary arrangements for that?'

'Yes, of course.' The manager smiled at Cat. 'Please come through to my office.'

As Cat followed behind the men she noticed that, although

Antonio was tall, Nicholas still had the advantage of a few inches and he was also more powerfully built, his shoulders wide, tapering down to narrow hips. She liked Nicholas's body—liked the way it felt to be held by him. Realizing the direction of her thoughts, she frowned and hurriedly looked away. She really was going to have to stop thinking like this.

Once off the main hall, there were a few small boutiques selling jewellery and designer clothes. She glanced in the windows as she passed but there was no time to linger. The men stepped back, allowing her to enter the office ahead of them. And for the next hour there was no time to think about anything except her proposals for the campaign.

She was impressive in business, Nicholas thought as a little later they went through to the ballroom to assess the strategic elements of how the advert could work. He watched as she stood in the centre of the dance floor and looked around the baroque interior with undisguised excitement.

'This is fabulous,' she breathed. 'It will be perfect for what we were discussing. You can almost sense history in here.' She glanced up at the high ceilings and the walls, decorated with gold leaf and elaborate frescoes. 'Do you still host masked balls in here?' she asked Antonio.

'Oh, yes, in Carnival time, which is just before Lent, we have many evenings of masquerade balls. You should come, the historical costumes are magnificent and you—if I may be so bold—would look ravishing in one, don't you think, Nicholas?'

Cat caught the sardonic glitter in Nicholas's eyes at the comment and blushed. 'Well, thank you, Antonio,' she hurried on, returning the focus of conversation firmly back to business before he could reply. 'I was thinking that we could film a few people in costume at strategic places around the hotel—' She wished Nicholas wouldn't watch her so closely. He made her nervous—he also made her intensely aware of the fact that she wasn't wearing any underwear. 'Em…linking in with what we were er…discussing in the office.' She glanced down at her notes and tried to gather her senses. 'We should take a look at one of the master suites next. I think if we—'

'We will go up there now, Catherine, as I think we have detained Antonio long enough.' Nicholas had been leaning almost indolently against one of the pillars in the room but he detached himself from it now to walk forward. 'I've requested my private suite to be prepared for us. We will take dinner there and conclude this conversation.'

Cat felt her heart thump with nervous anticipation. She was desperate not to be left alone with Nicholas, but Antonio was already taking his leave, assuring them of his utmost assistance for the plans they had been discussing. 'Let me know when you have finalized your decision on this, Nicholas. And meanwhile may I wish you both a pleasant evening.'

'Alone at last,' Nicholas said mockingly as the hotel manager strolled away. 'I think you made yourself a conquest there.'

She ignored the observation. Antonio probably treated every woman with the same level of charm. 'You shouldn't have been so quick to dismiss him,' she said instead.

'You think so?' Nicholas's eyes blazed with heat for a moment. 'Well, you will have to contain your disappointment, Catherine.'

The derisive words made her blush wildly. She glanced down at the notes in her hand. 'I meant that we still have rather a lot to get through,' she blustered. 'We could have used Antonio's input—for instance, these outdoor shots—'

'Right now my mind is focused on indoor pursuits.' His eyes met hers boldly as she looked up.

She hoped he was referring to taking dinner but somehow, just by the way he was looking at her, she doubted it. And, to her horror, she was aware that, along with the feeling of apprehension inside her, the heat of sexual excitement blazed fiercely.

Angrily she fought the sensation down. For the sake of her self-respect as well as her work she couldn't afford to let herself become used as just another conquest. 'Well, if you don't want to discuss the finer details of the advert any further, we should finalize the deal right now.' She raised her chin and met his gaze firmly.

An enigmatic smile curved the corners of Nicholas's mouth. 'Let's go upstairs, Catherine.'

The words were dangerously quiet. Go upstairs for what? she wondered frantically. To sign the deal—to have sex?

He stepped back, indicating with a rather imperious sweep of his hand that she should accompany him out. Cat hesitated, then, taking a deep breath, she walked ahead of him towards the door.

There was a lift directly outside the ballroom and the doors were open as if waiting for them. As they stepped inside, Cat was reminded forcefully of the first night they had met.

She watched as he pressed the button for the top floor and snippets of conversations played mockingly through her mind.

A sexual heat exists between us, Catherine. We've both known about it very forcefully since the first moment our eyes met.

Her eyes collided with his for a second and she could almost hear his voice.

This is inevitable, because the truth is that you want me as much as I want you.

Hurriedly she wrenched her gaze away from him. This wasn't inevitable, she told herself fiercely—she would remain aloof and she *would* concentrate on business.

The lift opened and Nicholas led the way down a richly carpeted corridor to open a door at the end. Then he stepped back to allow her to precede him inside.

The room that Cat entered was exquisite. Whereas the suite at Nicholas's London hotel had been ultra-modern in design, this one was completely in keeping with the character of the hotel, baroque yet lavishly elegant. They were in a lounge area and the Venetian glass chandeliers sparkled over gold-leaf antique furniture and heavily brocaded sofas. Outside on a terrace overlooking the floodlit beauty of the city, a candlelit table was laid for two.

Cat put her briefcase down on one of the side tables and tried not to look through the door that led towards an enormous four-poster bed draped in white muslin and rose-patterned chintz.

They were the most romantic surroundings she had ever seen, and the perfect setting for seduction.

But she wasn't going to allow herself to be seduced, she reminded herself firmly. 'I took the liberty of bringing along a contract for you to sign. It's for the first three adverts.'

'Did you indeed?' Nicholas sounded amused.

The fact that her attempt to be businesslike somehow amused him galled her deeply, and somehow that anger helped to suppress the weak feelings of inevitability as she turned to look at him.

'Don't patronize me, Nicholas,' she said quietly. 'I've come here to discuss business with you. And you promised me an answer before the end of the day, as I recall.'

'Yes, I did, and I am a man of my word.' His dark eyes held hers steadily. 'But the day isn't over yet.'

Her hands curled into tight fists at her sides. 'Why are you—playing with me like this?'

He smiled at that.

'So what's the score, Nicholas?' she whispered huskily. 'I give myself to you and in return I get the contract for the commercial? Is that how you do business?'

As soon as the words left her lips she regretted them. They conjured a scornful anger in his eyes that lashed against her raw senses.

'Sorry to disappoint you, Cat, but no, that is not how I do business.' There was harsh derision in those words. 'If you remember, I was the one to insist we got business out of the way before we enjoy ourselves, but maybe that kind of strategy is more your style?'

He watched her skin flare with furious heat. 'How dare you suggest that?'

He had to admit that he liked her tenacity, liked the way her head tilted upwards and her eyes flared with almost regal pride. Was she capable of using all of her charms including her considerable beauty, to get what she wanted? Probably, he conceded grimly. She *was* considering marriage purely to get her hands on her inheritance, he reminded himself—she was a McKenzie. She was a woman.

'A word of warning,' he said smoothly. 'Don't dish out what you can't take.'

Cat's eyes blazed with fury and for a moment she just wanted to turn around and leave the room. She took a deep breath and forced herself to calm down. Running away wasn't going to get her the contract—and she supposed she had hurled the first insult. 'Are you going to sign this contract?'

'No, I'm not.'

The cool words hit her like a blow to her solar plexus. Deep down she had been so sure that he liked her ideas—in fact this evening she had almost taken it as a foregone conclusion that they would be going ahead. 'Why not?'

'Because the contract you have with you is for a series of three different commercials and, as I stated specifically from the beginning, I want to walk with this idea before I run.'

'Oh!' She felt her body relax and relief pound through

her. He wasn't telling her he didn't want the campaign, just that he didn't want to make such a big commitment to it—yet. 'Well, I did bring a contract solely for the first advert—just in case.'

'Very wise.' He shook his head and came closer to her and she could see a grudging respect for her in his eyes. 'You make a worthy adversary, Catherine McKenzie.' As he spoke he reached out and touched her face.

A worthy adversary—she didn't think he was referring to business now, but to the fact that she was probably the first woman in a long time to try to resist him. He viewed her as an opponent to be conquered and, judging by the gleam in his eye, he also now assumed because of her weakness earlier this evening that the battle was over.

'Well, I would advise that you don't underestimate me,' she breathed softly.

'Oh, I can assure you that I have no intention of doing that.' Something about the way he was touching her and the huskily soft words struck a chord inside her. His eyes locked with hers before moving hungrily towards her mouth. And suddenly unwelcome thoughts were plundering through her mind. She didn't want to be his adversary... She wanted to be as close to him as she could get... *She wanted him so badly it hurt*—

Swiftly she closed the torture of her needs away. She wasn't going to be driven by sexual desire into surrendering her control. No man—and certainly not one as arrogantly confident as Nicholas Zentenas—was going to exert that power over her.

Hastily she pulled away from him. 'We need to get this wrapped up.' She turned to search blindly through her briefcase. 'I have the relevant contract somewhere in here,' she mumbled.

Nicholas noticed that her hands weren't at all steady and he smiled to himself.

'Ah, yes—here it is.' She pulled out a file like a conjurer. 'Do you want to read it?'

He laughed at that. 'Of course I want to read it.'

'It is all in order.' She watched as he calmly took it from her and scanned the details.

Silence descended and she found herself holding her breath. This was what was important to her, she told herself fiercely. This would be her first major deal and so, hopefully, the beginning of a more settled phase in her life—a flourishing career away from her family, her debts little by little repaid and, most of all, complete independence.

'Have you got a pen?' He asked quietly after a moment.

Their eyes met and she smiled. Then hastily she turned to scrabble in her bag to find one.

He signed the contract with a flourish and then a copy for his records. 'Good, now our business is successfully completed.'

'Well, the first part of our business,' she corrected him hastily. She still needed the rest of the campaign.

Amusement gleamed in his dark eyes. 'I'm glad you reminded me about that.'

There was suggestive warmth in his voice that wasn't lost on her, but she tried to pretend that it was. 'And now we can head straight back to the airport,' she continued hastily and turned to lock the paperwork safely away.

'We could, but I don't think we will,' he said softly. 'As you said yourself, we have unfinished business.'

'Nicholas, I—'

Whatever she had been about to say—and really she wasn't even sure—was cut off by the fact that he moved closer in behind her and put his hands firmly on her waist. The feeling was provocative and firmly proprietorial. 'Why are you trying to pretend that this afternoon didn't happen, Catherine?'

The whispered question against her ear made her senses pound.

'You wanted me,' he reminded her teasingly. 'In fact you begged for me.'

The reminder made her flush with heat.

'Do you know what I think?' His tongue licked at the sensitive cords along her neck. 'I think you are frightened by the way I make you—feel.'

'I'm not frightened of anything,' she lied fiercely, but the remark was so accurate that it was scary.

'You like to be in control and, when you're with me, that doesn't happen.' The lick of his tongue became a gentle butterfly kiss and at the same time his hands stroked firmly up over her hips in a way that pulled up her skirt.

She closed her eyes, fighting desperately against the sudden violent desire his caress unleashed. 'Please—don't, Nicholas!' To her disquiet the whispered words held more emphasis on the word *please*, making it sound more like an invitation than rejection.

He picked up on the weakness immediately. 'You mean please don't...stop.'

'Nicholas...' Her voice was a low groan of need now as his hand stroked up underneath her dress, finding the tops of her stockings and then smoothing upwards over the naked flesh of her hips and across the flat lines of her stomach before softly skimming downwards between her legs with ruthless concentration.

As his fingers lightly brushed against the moist heat of her sensitive core, her eyes flew open and connected with his in the ornate Venetian mirror directly facing her.

'I think we were about here this afternoon...weren't we?' His voice rasped against her ear, husky with sensual pleasure.

When she didn't answer him immediately, his fingers toyed

with her, making her quiver with a sharp, achingly sweet need. He watched the way she gasped and then caught the softness of her lower lip with her teeth to stifle the sound.

'You want me as much as I want you—don't you?' His voice was as tormenting as the fingers that invaded her wet softness. 'Surrender to me now, Catherine.'

'No!' The fact that he was watching her every reaction in the mirror made her feel overwhelmingly helpless. His touch lightened as if he might pull away from her and she gave an involuntary sob of need. 'Yes...don't stop!'

'Not quite clear enough. Tell me how much you want me.'

Her dress was now completely hitched up around her waist and, as he held her back against him, she could feel his erection through the linen of his trousers, pressing against her bottom.

She fought against saying those words and, to her mortification, he lightened his caresses even more until her whole body screamed out in need for him to continue. 'All right, you win.' She turned her head away from her reflection; she couldn't bear to witness how weak she was. 'You know that... I want you.'

She heard her dress rip as it was forcibly tugged down and then his other hand found her breasts, jerking down the lace of her bra so that they were pushed upwards, nakedly inviting his eyes to rake over their throbbing peaks.

'You are so beautiful.'

There was a momentary splinter in the harsh tone, a note that she caught and held on to because with it came a measure of empowerment. OK—he'd won, she acknowledged. She had been lying to herself when she had told herself she wasn't going to give in to this. The fact was she was desperate for him and her surrender was now unconditional. *But she wasn't the only one who had lost control.*

Her eyes flew to his in the mirror and she saw the fierce

blaze of need in the dark depths and smiled. Sensuously she moved her hips and rubbed herself against him, feeling him strain against the tight constraints of his clothes.

'Why, Nicholas, the steely control is slipping.' She almost purred the words, her satisfaction intense as she saw the dark eyes narrow. *She liked this power!*

She lifted her arms and wound them back around his neck, stroking her fingers through the dark thickness of his hair. The movement lifted her breasts even further and she heard his sharp intake of breath. 'Maybe you should be the one surrendering to me,' she suggested playfully.

'I knew you were a witch, Catherine McKenzie.' He growled the words out in a ragged tone as she turned to face him. Coolly she stood before him and unzipped her dress so that she could step out of it properly. Then she took her bra off and dropped that on the floor. All she was wearing now were the silk hold-up stockings and her high heels. For a moment she stood quite still, inviting his gaze.

His eyes ravished her body with hungry intensity. She had the most incredible figure, her breasts full and firm and her waist tiny before flaring out to the womanly curves of her hips. His gaze lingered on the triangle of gold hair between her legs before drifting down over their shapely length.

'You like what you see...don't you?' Calmly she reached out, allowing her fingers to stroke over his erection and unfasten the zip of his trousers.

The size and strength of his arousal made her heart start to race with anticipation. 'Maybe you should be the one saying please to me,' she whispered tremulously as she knelt down in front of him and touched the tip of her tongue against him.

'Why don't you try it—please—Cat?' With each word she took him into the warmth of her mouth.

Nicholas felt a piercing thrust of need; he closed his eyes

against it but it was violent and insistent and the force of the intensity shook him.

She looked up at him, a secretive smile curving her lips. 'I'm waiting for you to tell me how much you want me.' She whispered the words and allowed her breasts to brush against him playfully.

Suddenly a red mist of need seemed to possess him. 'I've got a better idea.' He took a deep shuddering breath as he strove to take back his control. 'Let me show you instead.'

Before she realized his intention, he caught hold of her and, scooping her up into his arms, strode through to the bedroom.

For a moment panic gripped her as her control over events vanished.

'Nicholas, I…'

He wasn't listening; he was undressing and then snatching back the covers of the bed to fling her down against silken sheets.

'Nicholas!' She stared up at him, wide-eyed, and for a moment excitement gave way to fear. Maybe she shouldn't have teased him…maybe she should tell him that she had never done this before…maybe…maybe…

But it was too late for talking. He straddled her with a fierce determination and parted her legs with his knees.

She was pinned down and helpless. A smile curved his lips now as his hand trailed down over her, his thumbs grazing against her swollen nipples. 'That's better.'

Their eyes met and held. 'Now, Catherine, I will teach you how to submit properly to me…' He spoke in Greek and as he did so he rubbed his erection over the wet softness between her legs. His hands moved to pin her wrists to the bed and then suddenly he bent and kissed her. She expected the pressure of his lips to be fiercely demanding but by contrast it was a gently provocative kiss, almost tender in its assault on her senses. She kissed him back hungrily, opening her mouth for his tongue. He let her hands go and her arms moved to twine around his neck, so that she could pull him closer and hold him.

His hands stroked down over her body and as he pulled back to look at her she smiled at him. This felt so *right*.

He moved her legs further apart with his knee and then suddenly he was inside her.

It hurt and she cried out involuntarily. She closed her eyes against the pain as he started to move and his name was just a gasp on the softness of her lips.

'Catherine—are you all right?' Instinctively he eased back for a moment. And, as their eyes met, she realized that despite the pain she didn't want him to stop. She wanted the full force of him—wanted him beyond reason.

'Yes…'

He stroked his hands over her body and she squirmed with pleasure. 'Oh, Nicholas…yes.'

Then he drove deeper into her, taking her shuddering gasps with his mouth, plundering her lips and the inner core of her mouth with brutal passion. She wanted to cry as pain turned magically to pleasure.

His hips moved against her and she writhed sensually beneath him. She wanted this feeling, this need, to go on and on for ever but it was rising insistently to a crescendo, ebbing up and up like an underground spring about to transform into a waterfall.

She sobbed his name as the release came flowing through her, sending her body into spasm after spasm of pure ecstasy.

He jerked against her as finally he allowed himself to follow. And for a while they clung together, swept away by the feeling. Cat's head was buried against his shoulder, her arms wrapped around him, holding him tight.

He pulled away slightly to look down at her.

Cat didn't want him to say anything; she didn't even want to think too deeply—she just wanted to luxuriate in the afterglow.

She reached up and stroked her hands through his hair, her eyes moving over the handsome contours of his face, lingering on the sensual curve of his lips. As if reading her mind, he leaned closer against her and kissed her deeply. It was a kiss unlike anything that had come before; it was so sweetly passionate that it made her want to cry.

Nicholas held her tenderly for a moment, his hand stroking down over the long length of her spine. He'd taken a lot of women to bed over the years but this had been the most incredible experience. He'd never wanted someone so intensely before; she had driven him into almost a state of delirium. Even now, holding her close, breathing in the scent of her perfume, feeling the warmth of her sensational body, he was aware that he wanted her again.

He frowned. This wasn't supposed to happen. He was supposed to leave her wanting more, not the other way around. Nicholas pulled away from her abruptly and reached for his clothes. He'd forgotten to use contraception, he realized suddenly—that had never happened to him before. It wasn't even as if he had been unprepared—he had condoms in his trouser pocket. How could he have been so stupid?

She stretched languorously and the sensual movement made him remember exactly why he had got so carried away. 'You've got a beautiful body,' he murmured.

The coolness of his tone flayed her sensitive nerves and Cat was suddenly acutely aware of the fact that she was naked except for her stockings.

She watched as he raked a smoothing hand through his hair and stood up. His eyes flicked over her nakedness and instantly she felt herself burn with desire. She still wanted him! The shame of that fact was like a punch striking into her. She had hoped that once she had surrendered to him she would be free of this need—that she could shake his control over her senses. But if anything her reaction to him now felt worse! She knew the pleasure he could give her and it was like some mind-altering drug that she desperately needed.

'You'll find a dressing gown in the *en suite*,' he told her nonchalantly. 'Put it on and come through to the terrace. I'll ring down for room service and we'll have dinner.'

She didn't want to eat! In fact she didn't think she *could* eat! All she wanted to do was run away and hide. Unfortunately she wanted to hide from herself and her own feelings as much as from him, and that wasn't so easy.

Cat was glad that he didn't wait around for an answer. She watched as he strode through to the other room and then she fled for the sanctuary of the bathroom.

Ripping off her stockings, she turned on the shower and stood under its forceful jet, trying to scrub away the weak feelings that had invaded her.

Cat had always prided herself on being strong. Although the sham of her romance with Ryan had hurt her greatly, she had made herself face the reality and had brushed him away with stoicism. She had told herself that no man would ever get under her skin again—she was too sensible, too wary of the pitfalls for that. She had known that she was nothing like her father, but she had also convinced herself that she was nothing like her mother either.

The episodes from the past that in adulthood had taken on a horrible clarity had been alien to her.

Her mother crying alone in her room when her father had rung yet again to say he wouldn't be home that evening.

'It's just because I miss him,' she had told Cat brokenly when she had tried to comfort her. 'I love him so very much.'

And when he did come home her mother had been so

happy. She would spend ages getting ready for him, making herself beautiful.

Cat had never understood that. Why would an intelligent woman waste herself on a man who didn't love her? In a way it had made her angry. It had driven her forward with her fierce determination to be independent. It was why she had always held herself back from emotional and physical commitment. It was why she'd had no difficulty finishing with Ryan and not looking back.

But now, as she wrestled with these feelings for Nicholas, she understood for the first time how her mother had felt and realized that maybe she wasn't so different from her as she liked to pretend. And that scared her more than anything!

Cat squeezed her eyes tightly closed as tears threatened to fall. She couldn't allow herself to be weak—she just couldn't.

CHAPTER EIGHT

NICHOLAS paced up and down the terrace. Below him the majesty of Venice glittered in all its beauty, but he was blind to it. All he could think about was Cat and the way she had felt in his arms, the shuddering beauty of her body, the way she had looked at him with those mysterious and beautiful eyes.

His heart twisted. He had to stop thinking like this he told himself fiercely. Cat meant nothing—she was a McKenzie! Leaning against the stone balustrade of the building, he forced himself to remember exactly why he was doing this.

Nicholas's parents had died when he was three and he had been brought up in an orphanage on mainland Greece. The regime of the institution had been strict; there had been no love, no maternal influence, just the rigour of schoolwork and the ethic that to get anything in this life you had to earn it. By the time he had reached the age of ten he had given up on ever having a family life. Nobody really wanted to adopt a ten-year-old.

Then Stella and John Zentenas had walked into his life. From the moment they had first met, something magical had happened; straight away it was as if he really did belong somewhere. The day they had adopted him and brought him back to their home in Crete had been the proudest day of his life.

Although Stella and John had no children of their own, they both had large extended families who all lived in the same village. Suddenly, from having no relatives, Nicholas had cousins by the score, aunts and uncles and grandparents. And they had all shown him remarkable kindness and love, had embraced him and absorbed him into the community.

He had vowed to himself back then that he would never let them down—that he would repay their kindness, make them proud.

When Nicholas was nineteen his father had become ill and he had taken over the reins of his publishing business—a business that up until then had been struggling. Nicholas had always had a natural aptitude for figures—he had a shrewd brain and the Midas touch. Within a year profits had doubled, enabling him to buy his parents a new home with every convenience for his father's disabilities. Within two years the business had been worth a small fortune. He had advised his father it was time to sell and John had gone along with him. It had meant a very comfortable retirement for his parents whilst Nicholas had reinvested in other businesses—namely hotels—and the money had just kept pouring in.

In his mid-twenties Nicholas had taken a calculated risk to expand his small chain of hotels. For a while finances had been tightly stretched and it was at that time that the ancient olive groves that surrounded his village had been under threat from developers.

His uncle had come to him, asking him to help. The person who owned the land needed to sell and a developer had already approached him with a substantial offer, but he had plans for a housing estate that would rip the heart out of the countryside. There was land at the far side of the groves that would be ideal for a small hotel—could Nicholas step in and develop the area with sensitivity, giving the owner the money he needed whilst safeguarding their idyllic surroundings for the heritage of the village?

If the request had come even three months down the line, Nicholas could have bought the land outright and gifted it to the village without any development, but bankers had tied his hands. To finance the purchase he'd needed a partner, and a business partner obviously wanted profit. Developing a small hotel as his uncle had suggested seemed the only option as it meant the surrounding area could be preserved.

A banking associate had introduced him to Carter McKenzie and a partnership had been drafted.

Their business deal had been supposedly straightforward. Nicholas had made it clear that certain large sections of the ground were not to be developed and Carter had agreed to this without reservation. In fact he had heartily concurred that it would be almost sacrilege to destroy an area of such outstanding beauty. They had drawn up plans for a new hotel— plans that fitted the requirements. Then Nicholas had left Carter to oversee the project as he had business interests in the Far East that had needed urgent attention.

When he had returned a mere seven weeks later he had found the plans had been altered; the hotel hadn't even been started, but the ground that he had expressly promised to keep as greenbelt had been bulldozed and ripped out, ready for contractors to lay the foundations of a new housing estate.

Nicholas hadn't been able to believe what his eyes had told him and he would never forget returning home. The village where once his friends and family had welcomed him had been turned into a place filled with hostile stares and words of reproach. They had blamed him and he had blamed himself—but mostly he had blamed Carter McKenzie for lying to him and for trying to steal the two things that mattered to him most—his honour and his family.

Even when angrily confronted, Carter had just shrugged his shoulders. 'I've done you a favour. We will make much more money out of the deal now.'

'Money wasn't the main issue,' Nicholas had ground out furiously. 'You stood to make a hefty profit on the deal that we agreed. But instead you've decimated land, burnt ancient olive and lemon groves that went back generations and were important for a whole community.'

'Money is always the main issue,' Carter had sneered. 'I did what you didn't have the guts to do. You should be thanking me.'

'I gave my word to the community that this wouldn't happen,' Nicholas had said quietly. 'You know that.'

Carter had merely laughed.

Remembering that laughter strengthened Nicholas's resolve now. At the time the only thing he could do to put things right was to buy Carter out and luckily he'd been able to afford to do that as his Far Eastern hotels came on line.

But of course that had been Carter's plan all along. Their mutual acquaintance in banking had informed him that if Nicholas's gamble in the Far East paid off he would be a millionaire. Carter had then taken a calculated risk that Nicholas would be successful and deliberately he had started to destroy the land. Then he had sat back and waited, knowing that in order to reclaim the land Nicholas would have to buy him out. It had almost amounted to legalized blackmail and it had galled Nicholas to pay, but to reclaim the land before the builders moved in there had been no alternative.

However Nicholas had always sworn that one day he would make Carter McKenzie pay. He had watched from afar as he'd continued to go through life walking over people—extorting money. The man was without morals or principle. His son Michael was the same and so was his daughter.

He ran a hand through his hair and forced himself to look at the facts and forget the heat of their lovemaking, the warmth of her embrace. She was as guilty as her father, tainted by association, complicit in a major swindle only last year. He couldn't forget that—couldn't allow himself to be swayed from what he had to do.

There was a knock at the door. It was room service and he let them in and then watched as they laid out a selection of dinner dishes under the covered hotplates out on the terrace.

'Thanks.' He tipped them, closed the door behind them, then went to see what was keeping Cat.

The bedroom was deserted and he could hear the shower running in the bathroom.

He began thinking again about how pleasurable their lovemaking had been. And then he found himself thinking back to earlier in the evening, remembering the way she had looked at him when they had stood side by side on the jetty waiting for the water taxi. He had imagined she looked pure—like a girl afraid to trust, afraid of her emotions.

But that had just been a trick of the moonlight—hadn't it?

For a moment he thought back to the earlier events in this suite, analysing—dissecting.

Surely Cat hadn't been a virgin?

No! He shook his head as he remembered how she had saucily turned the tables to torment him—kneeling before him, kissing him, her eyes flashing with provocative fire.

Then later, as he had carried her through to the bedroom, she had been sensationally wild, there had been nothing timorous or even mildly restrained about her responses. Except when he had first entered her—she had cried out. The memory crystallized in his brain like a snapshot of time. Now that he thought about it, she had tensed enough for him to pull back slightly. Had he hurt her?

He sat down on the edge of the bed and felt shaken by the idea. Cat McKenzie couldn't have been a virgin—could she? Confusion muddied his clear views of what she was.

His assessment of her as a conniving siren sat awkwardly alongside the fact that she might have been a virgin. With determination he stood up from the bed and headed for the bathroom.

'Cat, can I come in?' He knocked loudly on the door.

'I'm in the shower. I'll be out in a minute.' Cat turned her head up to the water, allowing it to wash the tearstains from her face. She had to take charge of her emotions—she was stronger than this!

It was a shock when the door of the shower was wrenched open. Her vision was blurred from her tears and for a moment Nicholas was just a dark silhouette against the brightness of the room.

'What on earth are you doing? I'd like some privacy, please. I told you I would be out in a moment.'

'I have something to ask you.'

She frowned, trying to work out what it was about his tone of voice that was different. He sounded brusque yet...off balance, somehow.

'Nicholas, go away!' She pushed her wet hair back off her face with an unsteady hand and rubbed at her eyes and then, as the watery blur started to focus, she was aware that his gaze was raking over her naked body with unrelenting, almost punishing appraisal.

Self-consciously she brushed a hand over the soapsuds that glittered against her skin. 'Whatever it is, it can wait,' she said tensely. 'I'll only be a minute.'

Nicholas ignored the request and instead he reached out and turned the water off.

His hand brushed against her breast as he pulled back and suddenly she was frighteningly aware that her heart was thumping now with a different emotion. She wanted him again.

Fury pounded through her senses, mingling with red-hot desire. She had to get rid of this feeling—get rid of Nicholas. She met his eyes defiantly.

'Are you a virgin?'

He ground the question out in such a way that she took an instinctive step back. Shocked, she stared at him, and for a few seconds there was a tense, unnatural kind of silence. Then she laughed—she didn't know if she was laughing because she was so nervous and appalled by the question or if she truly found it funny. 'Why are you asking me that?'

He held her eyes with a stubborn determination. 'Are you, Catherine?'

'How can you ask me that after what we've just done?'

'You know what I mean.' He wasn't amused. His dark eyes seemed to slice into her very soul.

'Pass me a towel, please.' Any pretence at amusement was now dead. She tried to avoid the question along with his eyes.

'Not until you answer me.' He sounded dangerously angry now.

'How dare you? It's none of your business what I am,' she flared.

He reached out and touched her face, tipping her chin upwards, forcing her to make the connection with his eyes. 'Answer me now,' he ordered softly.

'You've got a flaming nerve, Nicholas Zentenas. Just because we've had sex, it doesn't give you the right to barge in here, disturbing my privacy, asking personal questions.'

He didn't release her; in fact his grip was like iron, forcing her to maintain contact with his gaze.

She bit down on her lip. He was so arrogant and she wanted

desperately to tell him she had slept with hundreds of men. But she couldn't.

'I was a virgin.' She admitted the truth huskily. 'But it doesn't mean anything!' Her eyes flashed fire.

'Of course it means something!' His grip relaxed and then his thumb brushed over her lips, making her tingle with need.

She hated the fact that he could do that to her. Hated it with almost as much intensity as she loved it.

'You should have told me, Catherine—I'd have been more gentle.' There was a strange huskiness to his tone that she hadn't heard before. 'Did I hurt you?'

'No!' Her heart thumped uneasily against her chest. But he could hurt her... Oh, so easily he could emotionally destroy her... She acknowledged the truth to herself quietly. She needed to take back some control; she needed to drive him away.

'Why didn't you tell me?'

She took a deep breath. 'Because you might have thought it made you special. And it doesn't. It was just sex.'

The coldness of her response made Nicholas shake his head. The kitten had very sharp claws indeed. She was well able to look out for herself. 'I'm sorry to disappoint you, but I think it does make what just happened between us pretty special.'

'Don't be so sure of yourself, Nicholas.' Her voice trembled alarmingly. 'I got carried away...' She struggled to find an excuse for her actions and failed.

'You'd just signed your first major business contract and it was a powerful aphrodisiac, is that it?' He supplied the reason dryly as some of the certainties about her character slipped back into place. He'd been taken in by a beautiful woman once before—and it had led to the divorce court. He wasn't going to be duped a second time.

The suggestion stung but it was better than looking weak,

so she forced herself to hold his gaze mutinously and just shrugged. 'I suppose so.'

In a way he was relieved—it absolved any guilt that had momentarily assailed him.

'That's fine because I wasn't expecting anything deeper.' As Nicholas grated the words he was surprised to feel a flare of anger inside himself that he didn't fully understand. 'But one thing I'm certain of. No matter what has sparked it, there is a powerful chemistry between us. I'm the one who has awakened your sexual appetite. I'm the one who is going to teach you all there is about making love.'

'It was sex, not love-making, and it's not going to happen again.' She angled her chin up with fierce determination.

He laughed at that but it held a raw edge. 'It's going to happen whenever I want it to happen.' As if to illustrate the fact, he ran his hand down from her chin, over the glittering suds on her body, smoothing over the satin wetness of her breast, feeling how she instantly tightened beneath his fingers, her nipples hardening to throbbing peaks. 'You see!' He felt a flare of triumph mixed with arousal.

With difficulty she forced herself to flinch from the touch but the desire he had stirred up inside her was still vehemently insistent. 'That doesn't prove anything. Go away, Nicholas!'

He smiled and for a moment she thought he was going to comply as he reached and flicked on the water again. Then he started to unbutton his shirt, a look of deliberation in his dark eyes.

'What are you doing?' Her voice raised in alarm.

'What does it look like?' he drawled sardonically. 'I'm going to join you.'

'Nicholas, don't!' Her heart thudded fiercely as he dropped his shirt on the bathroom floor and then reached to take a condom from the back pocket of his trousers before unzipping them.

He had the most magnificent body—a bronzed, strongly muscled, smooth torso that tapered down to narrow hips and an absolutely flat abdomen. His erection was enormous and she averted her eyes from it hastily, her skin tingling with searing heat.

'This isn't a good idea,' she breathed huskily as he stepped into the cubicle beside her, but her voice lacked conviction now.

'Whether you like it or not, you want me, Catherine. So your body belongs to me right now; you may as well stop fighting the fact.'

There was determination on his handsome face as he moved forward and she backed against the tiled wall.

Water pounded down over them as he bent his head and captured her lips with his. The kiss was sweetly searing and it made her stomach turn over with longing. He could kiss so well, she thought hazily.

Almost of their own volition, her arms went up and around his shoulders. His hands smoothed over her, drawing her closer, then holding her bottom he pressed himself against her.

She groaned with need, kissing him urgently now.

'I thought you said this wasn't a good idea?' he teased her softly as he pulled back a little, his eyes gleaming with hunger.

'Well, I was wrong.'

Smiling, he reached to open the condom packet. 'This time I'd better be a little more responsible...hmm?'

She shuddered with desire as he lifted her off her feet and, holding her back against the shower wall, peppered her face and her neck with kisses whilst his hands stroked over her body with sensuous caresses. He was right, she thought dazedly. The chemistry between them was too intense. She didn't understand why he made her feel like this; all she knew was that she couldn't fight it. Even when he entered her, it was as if she still couldn't get close enough to him.

Despite the strength and the force of his passion, he was infinitely gentle and she wound her legs around him and gave herself up to the bliss of the feelings he could conjure up.

His hands cupped her bottom squeezing her against him, gently rocking her. She raked her fingers through his wet hair and tried to stop herself from crying out with ecstasy.

'I want you so much.' The words burst out of her uncontrollably with the feeling.

'Do you want to come?' He whispered the words huskily, his tongue licking against her earlobe, then lower down her neck.

'Yes…yes.'

He thrust into her with a passion that made her senses spin and her body convulse with delicious waves of sensuous pleasure.

She hadn't thought it possible for the feelings to be more intense than they had been the first time around, but they were. It was so earth-shattering that she wanted to cry tears of sheer joy.

He waited for her pleasure to spiral out of control before joining her, thrusting into her deeply, alleviating his desire with a forceful intent that turned her on all over again.

Breathless and spent, she clung to him under the jet of water. She wanted to be held like this for ever, with his heart thudding against her breast and his lips nuzzling against her neck.

Nicholas frowned to himself as he realized that once again he had completely lost control.

'Every time you touch me I seem to lose all perspective.' She whispered the words almost to herself.

He smiled. 'You can't fight chemistry. We may as well just let the sexual heat play out between us.'

The deeply taunting voice hit the rawness of need inside her.

'Are you hungry?' he asked suddenly.

'Not really.' She didn't want him to let her go but he was already pulling away from her.

'Well, I have to tell you I'm starving.' He lifted his head to the stream of water and let it wash over him. For a second her eyes raked over the perfect symmetry of his features, drinking him in whilst his eyes were closed. She wanted to stand on tiptoe and kiss his eyelids, kiss his lips; she itched to reach out and touch him again. Instead she balled her hands into fists and forced herself not to move.

He stepped away from her, out of the cubicle, and wrapped a towel around his waist before holding a bath sheet out for her.

'Just leave it over the heated rail,' she said as she raised her face towards the jet of the shower again. 'I'll be out in a moment.'

'Don't be long.' He did as she'd asked and then padded through to the bedroom, closing the door behind him.

Well, she had done it again—so much for being strong, she mocked herself fiercely. So much for keeping him at arm's length!

Switching off the water, she stepped out of the shower and wrapped herself in the warm towel. She should really get dressed and demand to be taken home right now.

Except that she didn't really want to go home now! Cat closed her eyes as memories of the way he had taken her seared through her mind. He'd started something inside her, had stoked a flame of desire that was now raging out of control. And, worse than that, he knew it.

She'd done the one thing that she said she would never do—she had given a man the power to control her.

Of course she couldn't leave things like this. She needed to take that power back from him before she lost every scrap of her dignity. The only problem was that, right at this moment, she didn't have a clue how she was going to do that. Was Nicholas right? Was she just going to have to give up and stop fighting against this, let him make love to her whenever he wanted until the feelings—whatever they were—had burnt out?

As the steam cleared from the mirrors in the bathroom, she had a clear view of herself within the gilded frame. Her lips were swollen from his kisses, her eyes were over-bright with emotion. And she was filled with anger at allowing herself to be so stupid.

First thing she had to do was get dressed; at least that would be some measure of armour in her defence. Hurriedly she went through to the bedroom to find her dress. It was lying on the floor just outside the bedroom door and as soon as she picked it up she realized that she would never be able to wear it again. It was ripped along one side, prompting memories from earlier. How his impatience had excited her—how she had eagerly welcomed the forceful way he had torn it from her.

She bit down on her lip as she tried to close her mind to that and the fact that exactly the same had happened to her underwear earlier! The single item of clothing she had left was a bra! Her only option was to put on the white towelling robe that was hanging behind the bathroom door.

As armour went, it was lamentably poor. She could hardly march out of the hotel wearing nothing but a bra and a bathrobe!

It seemed that Nicholas held all the cards in this game. And it was just a game—she had no doubt about that. He was toying with her, enjoying the fact that in the end she had been powerless to resist him.

She hated him for that—but she hated herself even more.

CHAPTER NINE

NICHOLAS was uncorking a bottle of champagne when Cat walked out on to the terrace.

The first thing she noticed was that he had changed into a pair of faded denim jeans and a white shirt. She had never seen him dressed so casually. The attire suited him, made him look relaxed and impossibly handsome. She felt her pulses quicken in response and then quickly tried to quash the emotion.

'Where did you get the clothes?' she asked with a frown.

'I keep a spare wardrobe at all of my hotels. It saves time having to pack.'

'Very convenient,' she said dryly. 'I don't suppose you keep a spare set of clothing for—' she hesitated, not wanting to say the word *mistresses* '—your guests,' she finished lamely.

'Sorry, no.' His lips twisted in an amused grin. 'But you look good in the robe.' His eyes swept over her. It was a size too big for her and seemed to dwarf her slender frame. Yet on her it looked incredibly sexy. He noticed how her hair was drying in soft curls around her face and her skin was glowing from the heat of the shower—or was it from their lovemaking?

He found himself wanting to walk across to untie the belt of that gown and allow his hands to run over her naked body. He couldn't seem to get enough of her!

'Unfortunately my dress is torn so I wasn't able to put it on.' Her eyes were bright with emerald sparks of fire as she caught the sensuality of his appraisal.

There was a spark of anger in her voice and he noticed how she also raised her chin defensively. He smiled to himself. Even though he had proved to her that she was his for the taking, she was still trying to assert her control over the situation and against him. He had to admit that he admired her tenacity. She also excited him beyond reason.

'Well, don't worry about that.' He lowered his voice huskily. 'Because you don't need any clothes right now and I'll buy you some new things tomorrow.'

He watched as her skin flared with heat. 'I don't want you to buy me anything!' she blazed. 'I can buy my own things.'

'Whatever you say!' He raised his hands in surrender.

'And I want you to take me home,' she said, pushing her advantage, and was taken aback when he laughed.

'Do you?'

The sardonic question made her blush wildly. 'I just said so, didn't I?'

'Well, if you want to go home tonight I will, of course, arrange it,' he agreed smoothly. 'But first I think we should have something to eat.'

Cat was about to say that she didn't want anything but as he took the covers off the silver tureens the delicious aroma of pasta floated in the air and she realized suddenly that she hadn't eaten since early this morning.

'Let's see, what have we got?' Nicholas read the menu that had been left for them. 'To begin with, Seafood Linguine, spaghetti with artichokes and herbs or Penne Arrabbiata?'

'That does smell good,' she conceded as she came closer towards the table.

He pulled out a chair for her. 'Come, sit down and I'll get you something. What would you like?'

She hesitated for just a second and then complied. What was the point in starving herself? She couldn't go anywhere until she had sorted out the problem of her clothes. And Nicholas was obviously not going to arrange for her to get back to the airport until after he'd eaten. 'Some linguine would be nice, thanks.'

As he pushed in her chair he leaned down close to her. 'By the way, I meant it when I said you look great in that robe—very sexy.' His breath was close to her ear and she could smell the clean male scent of him and her senses leapt uncontrollably.

'Well, as I'm sure you say that to all your guests, I won't take it personally.' She was proud of how cool she sounded but when he kissed her neck she found herself turning to jelly.

'Not *all*,' he drawled teasingly. 'You are in a class of your own, Cat.'

As he turned away to get their food he was aware that there was an element of truth in that statement. Catherine was different from any of the other women he had dated in his life. For one thing, she turned him on so completely that when they made love he forgot everything—even the fact that this was all about revenge.

He frowned, angry with himself for even conceding the thought. It was true that she turned him on with an incredible force; just a smile or a certain look in her eyes was all it seemed to take to make him want her like crazy. But he had to remember she was naturally duplicitous and this was just sex. Once he'd taken her to bed a few times the novelty would wear off, he assured himself forcefully. Certainly by the time he had got around to taking the McKenzie inheritance she would be well on her way to being history.

He put their plates down on the table and sat opposite her.

'Would you like a glass of champagne?' Without waiting for her to answer, he leaned across and filled her glass.

'Thank you.'

Their gazes collided across the table. She saw the fierce intensity in his eyes and it made her shiver. What was he thinking? she wondered. That he had enjoyed his *release*? Deliberately she reminded herself of the insensitivity of his remark on the plane. She thought it would help her to detach herself emotionally from the effects of those sensually gorgeous dark eyes. But strangely the memory just hurt.

Swiftly she looked away from him, out towards the glittering beauty of the city. They had a fabulous bird's eye view whilst being completely private. 'It's lovely out here, isn't it?'

'Yes.' Nicholas's eyes were still on her face. How was she able to switch on that vulnerable look with such unerring precision? She wasn't vulnerable, he reminded himself fiercely. It was an act.

She was a true McKenzie—driven by business deals and money, nothing more. Yet, despite the assurances, he couldn't help but wonder about that look in her eyes and the fact that she had been a virgin.

'You know you should have told me that you hadn't slept with someone before.' He hadn't intended to bring up that subject again but somehow he couldn't leave it.

She looked back at him coolly. 'I thought I made it clear that I didn't think it was any of your business.'

'Pardon me for being old-fashioned, but when two people have been as intimate as we've just been, I think it was very much my business.'

'You are not old-fashioned.'

He couldn't help but smile at the assertion. 'Maybe you're right, but strangely, the fact that you chose to give your virginity to me intrigues me.'

'Because you view it as an ego boost.'

'No, because I view it as something special.'

There was an honesty about the way he said those words that tore at her.

'Don't, Nicholas.' It was as if he had found an open wound and pulled at it.

'Don't what?'

'Pretend.' For a second her eyes were almost pleading with him. It took him aback and he fell silent. 'Perhaps you are a bit flattered by the fact that I was a virgin—but you and I both know that nothing out of the ordinary is taking place here. You probably do this kind of thing every week with a different woman.'

He laughed at that. 'I can assure you I don't.'

She looked over at him, her eyes mocking him now.

'I'm not trying to tell you that I haven't been out with lots of women. Of course I have—but not a different one every week!' He smiled and shook his head. 'I've got to leave myself with enough stamina to get some work done, you know.'

The throwaway remark made her laugh.

She had a very attractive laugh, he thought distractedly; it seemed to light her eyes with warmth. If it were true that the eyes were the windows of the soul, then he had seriously miscalculated in his assessment of her.

The thought was not welcome. Why the hell did he keep thinking things like that?

'So tell me a bit about yourself,' he invited suddenly.

Instantly her wary expression returned. 'Why?'

He laughed. 'Why not? That's what two people do when they have dinner together for the first time—isn't it?'

'We don't have that kind of relationship,' she said quickly. She didn't want him pretending to be interested in her in any deep, meaningful way. Maybe she couldn't control the intensity of her responses when it came to making love with him, but she could guard her innermost self—at least that way she could keep her heart safe from him, keep some pride intact.

'Don't we?'

She shook her head. 'Any conversations we have should be centred around business.'

'We dispensed with business earlier.' His voice was dry.

'Not entirely,' she disagreed. 'We didn't actually get around to discussing the outdoor shots and whether or not the rest of the campaign should follow the—'

'Cat, the rest of the campaign hasn't been agreed on yet. And there is no point in discussing it until we've completed the first ad.' He bit the words out tersely. 'I've already made that quite clear. So stop trying to hide behind work.'

'I'm not trying to hide behind anything,' she said quickly. 'I'm simply saying that we need to at least keep future adverts in mind when we are making this first one.'

'Just leave it, OK.'

'If that's what you want.'

'It is.' He frowned and watched as she toyed with her food. 'What I want to talk about now is you.'

'There's not much to say on that subject.'

'I don't believe that.'

'Well, it's true.' She shrugged. 'I graduated from university earlier this year, found a job in advertising. That's it.'

'And you're—what—twenty?' He pretended to hazard a guess and she nodded. 'That's young to have graduated.'

'Is it?' Cat shrugged. She had always been focused. She had wanted to leave home as soon as possible, and in her mind qualifications had equalled independence so she had pursued them with alacrity.

'When are you twenty-one?'

'Just over three months.' She reached for her glass and took a sip of the champagne. Why was he asking these questions?

She didn't want him analysing her life—her reactions. And she certainly didn't want to discuss her birthday!

'Are you planning anything special?'

'No.'

'I suppose your family will be throwing you some kind of celebratory event?'

She shrugged and her eyes met his with a kind of stony indifference.

What had he expected? he thought angrily. She was hardly going to admit to the fact that she was considering a marriage of convenience to get her hands on her inheritance. But she could say something!

'But you do have a family?' he pressed. 'Didn't you tell me something earlier about having a brother who dotes on you?'

She took another few sips of champagne and felt the alcohol hitting her system. 'He's my half-brother. My mother died when I was young and my father married again.'

He already knew all of that, but at least she was giving him a piece of personal information at last rather than monosyllables.

'And what about your father—are you close?'

She swept a hand through the length of her hair. 'He's my father—what do you think?'

He frowned. 'Well, fathers usually adore their daughters, don't they? So I presume you're Daddy's girl. Spoilt rotten and his adoring number one fan.'

'Absolutely.' She took refuge behind the illusion and smiled at him.

The candlelight flickered and danced as a warm breeze suddenly disturbed it, but not before he had witnessed the intense glitter in the beauty of her eyes.

She was obviously very defensive about her father; maybe people had openly criticized him in the past and she had built up a natural antipathy to anyone delving too deep.

It stood to reason. If she didn't adore her father and her brother she wouldn't go along with their crooked schemes. He didn't know why he kept feeling these momentary pangs that he was wrong about her. He'd had her checked out thoroughly by his private investigator. He knew what she was like.

'What about you?' She switched the subject hurriedly before he could ask anything else. 'Have you got any family?'

'Yes, like you, family is very important to me.' His eyes held hers steadily. 'My father died some years ago, but my mother and extended family all live in the same small village in Crete where I grew up.'

The sudden insight made her look at him with renewed interest. Because he was so wealthy and powerful, she had assumed that he would be too busy making money to have much time for family affinity.

'And what about children; did you have a family with your ex-wife?'

'For a woman who only wanted to talk about business you've suddenly changed your tune.'

The mocking tone made her withdraw instantly. 'I was just curious.' She shrugged.

'Well, in answer to your question—no, we had no children. Probably just as well, seeing as the marriage only lasted six months.'

'I'm sorry.'

The gentleness of her tone made his lips twist derisively. He didn't want a McKenzie's sympathy. 'Don't be. Sylvia was no great loss.'

There was an edge of rawness about the statement that made Cat frown. Had his ex-wife managed to cut through that haughty exterior? Had she dented his pride and hurt him? For a second she wanted to believe that because it made her understand why he seemed so remote sometimes. She knew what it was like to feel rejected—she'd felt like an outsider in her own home for nearly all of her childhood. She knew what it was like to have your feelings trampled into dust, how wary it made you of people and how much it hurt, and it made her want to reach out to him.

Then, as she met the harsh, almost ruthless expression in his eyes, she quickly blocked out the thought. Reaching out emotionally to Nicholas Zentenas would be as stupid as reaching out to a man-eating tiger.

This was the problem when you slept with someone, she told herself furiously. It was all too easy to start trying to attach real feelings to the situation, to start reinventing your lover's persona, distort reality.

Well, she wasn't going to be that stupid!

He watched as she put her cutlery down. She hadn't eaten much. 'Shall we move on to the main course?' he suggested. 'I think there's—'

'Actually, I couldn't eat another thing,' she cut across him quickly. 'I'd prefer it if you would just arrange for me to head back to the airport.'

He sat back in his chair and regarded her steadily. 'I take it you don't mind travelling back dressed as you are?'

'Don't be ridiculous.' She glared at him. 'I thought we could phone one of the boutiques downstairs. I'll have to buy something new.'

He glanced at his gold wristwatch. 'Cat, it's late. The shops are closed.'

She felt a rising sense of panic. 'Yes, but you could get them opened if you wanted.'

'I don't think so. The staff will have gone home.' He got up and cleared the dishes from the table, then placed a bowl of strawberries down between them.

She watched him through narrowed eyes as he sat back in

his chair. 'You never had any intention of getting me back to London tonight, did you?'

He shook his head. 'But I'm a man of my word. If you really want to leave, I'll arrange for my jet to be on standby and a water taxi to come and pick you up.'

'In a dressing gown!'

'Well, as I already said, there's nothing I can do about that.' He nonchalantly reached out and picked up one of the strawberries. 'You should try these; they are lovely with the champagne.'

'I don't want anything, Nicholas.'

She had no doubt that if he wanted to get the boutiques downstairs reopened he could make one phone call and it would be magically arranged. She had a good mind to call his bluff and tell him to go ahead and make the travel arrangements for her.

'Shall I tell you what I want?' he asked quietly.

When she made no reply he smiled.

'I want to spend the whole night making love to you.' He said the words softly as he met the shimmering intensity of her eyes. 'I want to kiss you all over, hold you in my arms and take you over and over again.'

Something about the way he said that made her heart turn over with longing. He watched the heat rise in the creaminess of her skin and laughed. 'And I think that is what you want too.'

'You are an extremely arrogant man, Nicholas,' she murmured angrily.

He smiled and reached out to touch her hand. 'But you want me as much as I want you—why do you keep fighting against this truth?'

'I'm not fighting against anything,' she lied breathlessly. His fingers ran softly over her hand, stroking against the inside of her wrist and stoking her senses almost absently.

How was it that he could turn her on so effortlessly? She closed her eyes for a moment and strove to find some sense within the torrent of emotion. It was just sex, she told herself fiercely. As long as she recognised that, he couldn't reach her on an emotional level and therefore she would be safe. 'But I guess I'm stuck here, aren't I, seeing as you ripped my dress.' She tried to make her voice indifferent as her eyes snapped open.

He smiled and she tried to ignore the gleam in his eyes that told her he was not fooled.

'But tomorrow we should discuss business again,' she continued hurriedly. 'Sort out the outside shots and how we can carry the theme through to—'

'Cat!'

She broke off disconcertedly as he squeezed her hand. 'Yes?'

'Come over here.'

'Don't talk to me like that!'

He looked at her mockingly. 'You asked me not to pretend. But you are the one who is putting up the pretence. We moved on from the subject of work—remember?'

She shrugged, at a loss for what to say. Her eyes travelled from the searing power of his gaze to the way his hand held hers. The gentle touch of his skin against hers made her shiver with need.

'Are you cold?'

She laughed; the summer night was intensely hot, to say nothing of the way he made her feel. 'No, I'm not cold.'

'You're shivering.' He pulled her hand. 'Come over here.'

It was hard to ignore the order a second time because there was a gentler note hidden in the deep tone. He pushed his chair back and drew her around the table until she stood before him.

'That's better—you were too far away over there.' There was satisfaction in his voice as he caught her other hand and then pulled her down to sit facing him on his knee her legs either side of him. 'You're too tense, you need to learn how to relax.' He stroked a hand through her hair, brushing it back from her face so that he could see her more clearly. 'And I think I might just have the answer.'

'What would that be?' she asked huskily.

Their eyes locked.

'Maybe a few strawberries with champagne.' He murmured the words playfully as he slipped her dressing gown down and kissed her naked shoulder. 'And a little bit of this...'

The touch of his lips against her skin was wildly provocative. She closed her eyes as he worked his way higher, kissing the vulnerable curve of her neck.

'And a little bit of this...' He cupped her face and held her while his lips captured hers.

The feeling inside her was like a flame melting sweet chocolate. 'You are really bad for me, do you know that?' She whispered the words unsteadily as he released her.

'On the contrary—relaxation is very good for you.' His hands moved to the belt of her robe. 'It lowers the blood pressure.'

She laughed breathlessly as he untied the belt. 'That's definitely debatable.'

Why did everything feel right when she was in his arms? she wondered hazily.

This was a dangerous madness but she just couldn't resist him.

The dressing gown slithered to the floor and she looked up at the star-studded sky as his hands moved possessively over her.

It was easier to give in and infinitely more enjoyable than fighting him.

CHAPTER TEN

WHEN Cat woke up she was alone in the double bed. For a few moments she stretched out a hand towards the empty pillow next to her as she remembered the night of wild passion.

A strange ache seemed to curl in the pit of her stomach as she remembered the strong arms that had held her so tenderly, the whispered words of arousal and the possessive warmth of his kisses.

'Wake up, sleepyhead.' Nicholas came into the room and pulled back the curtains. Sunlight filtered across the room with a dazzling intensity.

'What time is it?' she murmured, putting a shielding arm across her face.

'Almost eleven.'

'Eleven!' Instantly she struggled to sit up, holding the sheet across her naked body with a measure of shyness that was absurd considering the fact that he had explored every inch of her with fervent concentration last night. 'I can't believe that I've slept so late!'

'Well, we were rather busy last night,' he murmured. 'Room service have sent up some tea.' He put a cup down on the dressing table beside her and she noticed that he was fully dressed in chinos and a white shirt. He looked suave and refreshed and by contrast she was suddenly aware of her dishevelled hair and sleep-smudged face.

'Thanks. You should have woken me earlier! How long have you been up?'

'I had a business call that I had to take at about nine. So unfortunately, I had to drag myself away—otherwise...' his eyes lingered on her creamy skin and the luxuriant mass of blonde waves on the pillow '...I would have definitely woken you up.' He smiled as he watched the rise of heat under her skin and the way she bit down on the rose-coloured softness of her lips—lips that were still slightly swollen from his mouth.

He felt a sudden urge to pull the sheet away from her and take her again. The impulse was stronger than he wanted it to be and, impatient with himself, he turned away. 'Drink your tea and then get dressed,' he murmured. 'I've had some clothes sent up to the suite for you. They are hanging on a rail outside in the lounge. Take your pick of what you want when you are ready.'

'Thanks.' His businesslike manner disconcerted her after the intensity of their passion last night. She didn't know how to deal with the situation. 'What time are we heading back to London?' she asked cautiously.

'I've spoken to the pilot this morning and he informs me that the first available air-space is six-thirty this evening.' He slanted a wry glance over at her. 'I know it is later than we had hoped, but unfortunately air traffic control has the last word on these matters, so it is out of my hands.'

'It will have to suffice, then,' she said quietly. But perversely she wished that there had been no available air space until the middle of next week. She also wished that Nicholas had sounded a little more enthusiastic about spending the day with her. The feeling was most unwelcome. What on earth was the matter with her? she wondered crossly. Last night she had at least attempted to think sensibly—now she wanted to stay here in a kind of limbo, luxuriating in his lovemaking, blocking out all logical, sane thoughts.

Get a grip, Cat, she told herself fiercely. They had enjoyed a pleasurable interlude last night—but it was unreal, it meant nothing to either of them and it certainly couldn't last.

The ring of the phone in the other room made him turn away. 'I'd better get that.'

'Yes, it might be important.' As the door closed behind him, she hurriedly gathered herself and got out of bed. She needed to shower and clear her head and then she needed to change the focus of her thoughts back towards work, she told herself firmly. As they were stuck here for a while, it was an ideal opportunity to consider some more ideas for the forth-coming campaign.

A little while later, showered with her hair dried into straight silken submission she looked around for the dressing gown she had worn last night—then remembered it was still out on the patio. For a second her mind stole back to the way he had made love to her out there under the bright starlit sky, candles flickering in the warm air as he'd slipped himself into her. Although she had been sitting on top of him, he had been the one in control, dominating her senses, making her writhe with need.

Hastily she snapped the memory closed as she felt the heat of desire flare up inside her all over again. It was over, she told herself fiercely. Time to move on.

Wrapping herself in one of the bath sheets, she cautiously stepped out into the lounge to look for the clothes Nicholas had left for her.

There was a rail just by the front door and, to her relief, Nicholas was out on the terrace talking on the phone, so she was able to flick through the clothes in privacy.

After she had got just halfway through the selection it

became clear that they were all designer labels and, although she couldn't find a price tag on anything, she was sure they would all be exorbitantly expensive and well out of her price bracket. They were gorgeous, though…and with each outfit there was a hanger with coordinated underwear, all in the correct size.

One summer dress in particular caught her eye; it was pure silk and the colour of the Caribbean sea on a summer morning.

She pulled it out and held it up to the light, admiring its iridescent sheen as the sun hit it.

'Strange you should select that dress.' Nicholas's voice from behind made her whirl around in surprise. 'It was the one that caught my eye too. I thought it would be stunning on you.'

'It's certainly very beautiful.' As he walked closer she tightly held the edges of the towel wrapped around her.

'You should try it on,' he suggested firmly.

'Actually, Nicholas, I don't usually buy designer clothes.' She put it back on the rail. 'They are beyond my budget.'

'They only sell designer labels here.' He reached behind her and pulled out the dress again, to hold it out towards her. 'Don't worry, I'll pick up the tab.'

When she still didn't take it from him, he shrugged. 'It's either that or go home as you are.'

Slowly she reached out a hand and took the garment from him. 'Well, I suppose I have no choice, then—but I will pay you back.'

For a moment he found himself captivated by the way she looked up at him. He had to hand it to her; she was a very good actress. There was a husky integrity about her tone, a light of clear principle in her green eyes. He'd have sworn that she really was uncomfortable accepting the gift and that she really wanted to pay him back. But then, to be successful at conning people you had to be a good liar—her father had been pretty plausible as well when he had agreed that it would be a felony to rip out the heart of a community.

'Don't worry about it,' he said dryly. 'I'll settle for seeing you in the dress—oh, and in these.' He picked up some blatantly seductive underwear and hooked it over the hanger of the dress. 'That will be payment enough.'

He noticed how her eyes shadowed as if he had struck her and against his will he wanted to reach out and gather her into his arms.

'I said I'd pay you back and I will,' she said tightly. 'And I won't be needing these…' She put the basque and the silk stockings back where he had taken them from and then, with her head held high, she marched back into the bedroom and shut the door firmly behind her.

Cat was shaking as she flung the dress down on the bed. She couldn't describe it but there had been something in the cool glint of his eyes that had struck her like a whip against raw flesh. He'd just treated her as if she were nothing more than a concubine—someone to be used like a plaything.

How could he look at her like that when he had made love to her so tenderly last night?

Idiot! Cat berated herself fiercely as she struggled with unfamiliar emotions. She couldn't understand why she was allowing him to get to her like this. Of course last night wasn't anything serious. But, that aside, she wasn't going to let him treat her like some kind of kept woman whom he could buy with a few trinkets and treat any way he damned well pleased. She had some self-respect left!

Strengthened by determination, she turned to pick up the dress. She had stepped into it and was just struggling to reach the zip when the bedroom door opened and Nicholas followed her in.

He cast his eyes over the long length of her back. It was

strange but he had never found a woman's back so incredibly erotic before. Something about the light golden tan of her skin made him want to run his fingers over her.

'Need some help?' he asked as he noted her struggle to reach the zip.

Blonde hair swished as she glared at him over her shoulder, her eyes like bright emerald splinters. 'No, thank you.'

Ignoring her words, he walked across towards her and took hold of her, one hand firmly at her waist whilst the other found the zip.

'What's wrong?' He whispered the words huskily against her ear as he ran the zip lightly up.

She closed her eyes, fighting the treacherous weakness that his close proximity always induced. 'You mean apart from the fact that you've just made me feel cheap?' she muttered sardonically.

'That wasn't my intention.' His hands lingered at the curve of her waist before sliding the zip all the way up, his fingers brushing provocatively against her skin. 'I ripped your dress last night, now I've replaced it. What's wrong with that?' He swept her hair away from her neck and kissed it softly.

Immediately she felt the rekindling of fire inside her. What was wrong with her? she wondered hazily. As soon as he held her and kissed her, everything was magically OK again! It was crazy.

'I'll tell you what's wrong with it.' She pulled away and turned to face him. 'You think because you've got money that you can buy anything you want—*anyone* you want. Well, I'm not for sale, Nicholas. I'm my own woman and I always will be.'

He smiled at that but it was a smile singularly lacking in humour. 'Actually, Catherine McKenzie, right at this moment you are *my* woman.'

She shook her head but her heart leapt as he took a step forward, his gaze hard and determined. 'And I can assure you I don't want to buy you.' She felt breathless as he reached out and touched her face, tipping it upwards so that his eyes could run over her with fierce intensity. 'I just want to possess you.'

The words sizzled through her consciousness with searing force. But before she could even formulate some kind of a reply he lowered his head and kissed her.

It was a hard, punishing kiss, yet it was so provocative and intense that she found herself melting and responding, returning it with a fierce need that tore through her very soul.

'I'm glad you didn't accept the underwear.' He growled the words against her ear as he pulled her skirt upwards, his hands possessively caressing her naked curves. 'I much prefer you without.'

Why did she let him do this to her? she wondered as she closed her eyes in sweet blissful submission. Why did she want him so much that nothing else mattered?

It was later in the afternoon before they finally ventured out of the hotel to go and have some lunch. The sun was sizzling down out of a clear blue sky and the waters of the canal looked an almost surreal turquoise against the backdrop of beautiful buildings.

Nicholas insisted that instead of waiting for a water taxi they took a ride in a gondola. 'You can't come to Venice and not take a trip in a gondola,' he said firmly.

'You are not going to turn all romantic on me, are you, Nicholas?' she quipped lightly.

He laughed and made no reply to that and immediately she wished she hadn't made the joke. What on earth had possessed her? Probably the same kind of madness that made her surrender to him every time he so much as brushed his fingers against her skin. Nicholas didn't want to have a romance with her—just sex.

She glanced away from him, stunned by how much it hurt when she reminded herself of these things. A gondola pulled alongside the jetty for the hotel and the gondolier held the boat steady, while Nicholas stepped down and reached to help her in. The boat rocked alarmingly until they sat down in the red velvet cushioned seat. Then the gondolier pushed them away from the platform and they glided smoothly out.

There was a good view of the hotel as they pulled back from it and Cat tried to concentrate on that rather than on the fact that, due to the close confines of the boat, she was pressed against Nicholas and his arm was draped across her shoulder, his fingers stroking absently along the bare skin at the top of her arm.

'The hotel looks fabulous from here,' she murmured. 'Maybe the outside shots for the advert should be taken from this angle.'

'Maybe.' Nicholas frowned and listened as she launched into a discussion on the merits of shooting the whole commercial with a soft focus lens. Cat was still an enigma to him. Sexually he had total control of her now; she was his for the taking and the passion between them was incredible. Yet as soon as he broke her barriers down, she deliberately started to rebuild them again. Why was that?

She should be ripe for reeling in now and yet she was still trying to twist away from him. He really hadn't foreseen this kind of problem. Usually when he took a woman to bed she wanted to curl up against him and turn the relationship into something deeper. Yet Cat seemed to deliberately seek a businesslike retreat.

It was a bit of a role reversal and it was very irritating. He was going to have to pull the strings a little harder, he thought decisively. He would get Catherine, hook, line and sinker, body and soul, if it was the last thing he ever did!

'Do you know what, Catherine? I really couldn't care less how we shoot the advert right now,' he cut across her firmly as she paused to draw breath, and his fingers ran upwards to stroke through her hair. 'All I can think about at the moment is how much I've enjoyed our time together here. In fact, you are having a very unusual effect on me.'

'Am I?' She slanted a curious look at him.

'Yes…' His eyes moved to her lips. 'The thing is, I can't seem to get enough of you.'

As he said the words Nicholas realized that they were true. Sexually speaking, she was driving him out of his mind.

'Don't say things like that to me, Nicholas,' she murmured huskily.

'Why not, when it's true?'

'I just… I don't want you to say things like that to me.' Her heart was thudding erratically against her chest as she met his eyes.

'What are you so frightened of?' He asked the question almost to himself.

She made no reply, but he could see the shadows of consternation in the beauty of her eyes. He frowned and ran a hand gently along her jaw, tipping her face upwards so that he could kiss her.

It was a tender kiss, unlike anything that had gone before, and it seemed to melt Cat's senses until she felt dizzy with need for him.

The gondola smoothly swished along the narrow maze of canals, under bridges, past houses and hotels. But for a while Cat was oblivious to everything except the pleasure of just being held and kissed. As the boat turned a corner out into the Grand Canal a breeze swept up and the waves were choppy. Some spray swished over the boat and they laughingly pulled apart. Then, without saying a word, she curled in against him again.

It was probably crazy but she couldn't remember ever being this happy before.

'You can see the Bridge of Sighs from here.' Nicholas pointed down one of the waterways. 'There it is.'

'It's beautiful, isn't it?' she said dreamily. 'Everything about this city is so perfect—it's like a romantic film set.'

'Yes, but appearances are deceptive. It's the bridge leading to the prison and it's called the Bridge of Sighs because the window was the last view a condemned man had of the city before incarceration.'

'I guess it's what you call reality—which is rarely romantic.'

'You are much too young and beautiful to be so cynical,' he said, laughing. 'Let me tell you, lots of romances have flourished in this city. For instance, it is rumoured that Casanova escaped from the prison to meet his one true love.'

'Casanova didn't have one true love,' she said with a laugh.

'How do you know that?' he teased. 'He just got really bad press. To coin a cliché, you should never judge a book by its cover.'

'You should never ignore the facts either—otherwise you could end up making a serious error of judgement.' She leaned her head back against his shoulder and tried to disregard the fact that she wanted to ignore the reality about Nicholas and believe that this was the start of something serious.

For a moment silence fell between them.

Was she starting to fall in love with him? As soon as the question entered her consciousness, she cast it away. She was enjoying his company—enjoying the intimacy of making love with him. *Nothing more.*

The boat glided smoothly in towards the shore.

'I hope you enjoyed that,' Nicholas said as he climbed out and reached to help her step on to dry land.

'Yes, it was great.' Cat avoided eye contact with him. Like

pebbles thrown in a pond, her thoughts had sent out disturbing waves that couldn't be ignored. She wasn't in love with him because she wasn't that stupid—for one thing, Nicholas would never return those feelings. She would never have the kind of life that she craved with someone like him; it could never be settled and ordinary. Women were just playthings to him.

So this wasn't love, but perhaps she was developing feelings for him and, if so, that was very dangerous territory. If she spent more time with him, those feelings could grow. Before she knew it, she could wake up one morning and be in love with him! Then her life really would be a mess.

She was going to have to finish this and the sooner the better.

They wandered along by the side of the water and she tried to think about the beauty of her surroundings and not what she had to do.

They turned a corner and walked into St Mark's Square; pigeons scurried and fluttered into the air against the impressive background of the basilica. A string quartet was playing classical music outside one of the pavement cafés.

Nicholas led her over to a table and summoned a waiter.

'You are very quiet, are you OK?' He looked across at her with that dark-eyed stare that seemed to cut straight through her.

'Yes, fine.' She tried to summon a smile.

He ordered champagne and then passed her a menu.

When they got back home he probably wouldn't even want to see her again. So she should reassert her independence. Finish this now, before he did.

She looked across at him and he smiled and suddenly she was backtracking. She couldn't do it now, she told herself violently. As soon as the plane touched down in London and they were back to reality—that would be the right time—that was when she would do it.

CHAPTER ELEVEN

CAT put some order forms down on her boss's desk and returned to the main office. It was raining outside; heavy slanting sheets of water were hitting the windows with a drumming sound. The heatwave had broken, summer was officially over and Cat's mood was as dark as the weather.

'There is a call for you on line two,' one of the secretaries informed her as she sat down at her desk.

'Who is it?'

'I don't know—they didn't say.'

Cat pushed a hand through her hair and tried to compose herself. Then, with a deep breath, she reached and lifted the receiver.

'Cat McKenzie here, how may I help you?'

'Oh, I can think of a number of ways you can help me, Catherine.' Nicholas's warm, teasing tone instantly made her blood run to fire.

Memories flicked through her mind—memories of how they had made love on his plane on the return journey from Venice. Memories of how, in the intervening weeks since that trip, she had been powerless to resist him. It seemed he just had to snap his fingers for her and she was there. She kept telling herself that she was going to finish things, but each time she spoke to him or saw him she put it off. She couldn't do it.

Then he'd informed her that he had to go away to Switzerland on business and she had convinced herself that he probably wouldn't return to London and that the affair was over. He'd been away for five days now, and as he hadn't phoned once, that certainty had grown. She'd tried to tell herself that she didn't care but just hearing his voice now made her realize what a lie that was.

'Hello, Nicholas, where are you?' Somehow she managed to make her voice sound coolly polite.

'I'm in London, at the hotel.'

'Was it a successful trip?'

'So-so. My work schedule has been a bit hectic. How about you? Have you missed me?'

The arrogance of the man still had the power to incense her. 'Well, like you, I've been a bit busy for that.'

'Sounds like we are both in need of some relaxation. Why don't I send the car over for you this evening and we'll have dinner at the hotel?'

He really thought that he could just pick her up and drop her at whim! Admittedly, over the past weeks, she'd agreed to see him many times—and had very much enjoyed the time they'd spent together. But she couldn't help thinking he'd had things far too much his own way for too long.

'Actually, tonight isn't good for me. I've got to work until seven; I have a few meetings and it's going to be pretty intense. I'll be fit for nothing except an early night when I get home.' It was true; she really did have to work late. The only pretence was the fact that she really would have given anything to see him afterwards.

'An early night sounds good to me,' he replied huskily. 'My driver can pick you up from your office.'

'And how is that going to look?' She lowered her tone and glanced around the open-plan office to make sure no one could hear what she was saying. 'I thought we'd agreed to keep our private life secret?'

'We did,' he agreed nonchalantly.

'Well, then, it's hardly going to be a secret if there is a great big white stretch limo outside the front door of the office waiting for me, is it?'

He laughed at that. 'Make something up. Tell anyone who asks that I wanted to see you to discuss the campaign.'

'And then my boss will want to know exactly what was said—and if, for instance, you've made up your mind about the follow-up adverts.'

'Tell her I'm thinking about it.'

'And are you?'

There was a slight pause. 'Not right now—no, I told you, I want to see how the first run of advertisements work out before going any further.'

'Well, that's fair enough, but I don't feel like drawing attention to the fact that you are thinking about it so hard. Let's just leave it tonight. I don't feel a hundred per cent well, anyway.'

'Why, what's the matter with you?'

'I'm just tired, I guess.' Cat glanced up as one of her colleagues approached her desk. 'Look, I've got to go; it's very busy in here. Ring me next week if you get time.'

She put the phone down.

'Cat, can you process these figures for me?' Claire put a stack of papers down in front of her.

'Yes—sure; when do you need them?' Cat was only half interested; her mind was going back over her conversation with Nicholas. Perversely she wished she hadn't put the phone down on him and that she had agreed to see him tonight. She really missed him. But that was pathetic—and she wasn't going to be like that, she told herself. Anyway it was true; people at the office would get suspicious if they saw Nicholas's car picking her up.

She had asked that they keep the affair secret because she had been concerned that it would reflect badly on her work—mixing business and pleasure wasn't encouraged—plus it might undermine the accomplishment of bringing in such a good client.

Nicholas had agreed without hesitation; in fact, he had added a few provisos of his own and suggested they keep the affair secret not only from her office but from friends and family too. 'It's best that way,' he had told her smoothly. 'Once the news is out that I'm seeing someone, the gossip columnists start getting involved and, before you know it, they will be printing stories about us, delving into your family background. Any privacy you had will be lost and sometimes it's not pleasant.'

It probably wasn't pleasant and she had agreed readily. She was an intensely private person anyway, and she certainly didn't want any scandal about her family and her inheritance circulating. But it was also very convenient for Nicholas. It meant he didn't have to introduce her socially; it meant that she was officially just a mistress.

She looked down at the papers in front of her and tried to concentrate. She felt a bit sick, but then that was nothing unusual—she'd been having bouts of nausea all week. There was obviously a bug going around the office. Claire had been off work all last week with it.

'Sorry, Claire, when did you say you wanted this?'

'You couldn't do it before our meeting tonight?'

Cat looked up at her drolly. 'That's not giving me much time!'

'I know.' Claire pulled a face. 'I'm sorry. I've had things on my mind.'

'Well, I suppose it's understandable. You haven't been well,' Cat conceded. 'Don't worry; leave it with me.'

'Thanks.' Her colleague smiled. 'Actually, Cat, you're looking a bit peaky yourself. Are you OK?'

'Yes, fine—although I think I'm coming down with a mild version of what you had last week.'

Claire blushed. 'I don't think there is a mild version of what I had last week.' She lowered her voice to a whisper. 'Unless there is such a thing as being a little bit pregnant.'

Cat looked up at her in surprise. 'You're not…are you?'

Claire nodded and put her finger to her lips. 'Don't say anything to anyone yet. I don't want it to be common knowledge around the office because it's early days.'

'Gosh! Congratulations. Claire.'

'Thanks. I have to admit it was a bit of a shock. I must have conceived on honeymoon. Like you, I thought I'd just got a bug. I was so tired and I kept being sick. Anyway, I bought one of those tests from the chemist and it's positive. Martin is so excited.'

'I'm really pleased for you,' Cat said sincerely.

Claire smiled. 'So is there something you want to tell me?'

'Sorry?' It took a moment for Cat to realize what she meant. 'Oh! No, I've just got a bug.' But even as she said the words, her eyes were flying towards the calendar on her desk. And she felt her heart start to thump against her chest with sudden and unequivocal panic as she realized that the joke might not be too far from the mark—her period was late.

It was still raining when Cat finished work. She stood in the Goldstein foyer and watched the water bouncing off the pavements. It was only a fifteen-minute walk to the underground station but she was going to get soaked. She debated going back to the reception desk to ring for a taxi, but on a Friday evening with the weather like this she could be waiting a long time. Plus she wanted to stop at the pharmacy down the road, which would involve leaving the driver with the meter running.

Pulling up the collar on her raincoat, Cat took a deep breath and hurried outside. It was dark and cold and the rain lashed against her skin with stinging force. Within a few moments her hair was plastered to her head.

She crossed over at the lights and hadn't gone very far when she realized that there was a vehicle drawing level with her. Glancing around, she saw it was Nicholas's limousine. An electric window wound down.

'Mr Zentenas has sent me to give you a lift, Ms McKenzie. Would that be acceptable to you?'

The situation and the chauffeur's polite offer seemed somehow bizarre in the middle of the ordinary street. She wanted to say no, it wasn't acceptable, that she had already told Nicholas she was unavailable, but the driver was so courteous that she refrained. 'That's very kind of you, but I won't if you don't mind. I have shopping I need to do now.'

'I can take you shopping. Mr Zentenas said I was to take you anywhere you wanted to go.'

'Before dropping me back at his hotel?'

'That was the general idea.' The driver shrugged. 'But I'm at your disposal, Ms McKenzie, and, if I may say so, you are getting very wet out there. Why don't you climb in and make yourself comfortable?'

She hesitated for just a second before nodding. 'OK, thank you.' What the heck? she thought as she opened the door and slid into the deep comfortable warmth of the heated leather seats. The driver was here now so she may as well take the lift.

Nicholas was sitting at his desk in the hotel suite. He had a mountain of correspondence still to get through, but Cat would be here soon and he wanted to check in with his private investigator before she arrived, so he put everything to one side and lifted the phone.

'Keith, it's Nicholas Zentenas.' He didn't waste time on preliminary small talk. 'Is there anything I need to know?'

'No, Mr Zentenas. Nothing. I've followed Ms McKenzie, as you asked. I've watched who comes and goes at the office and the flat and I've nothing to report.'

'So she hasn't met up with her father or her brother?'

'Her father is still in Germany on business. He is due back tomorrow. Her brother seems to be keeping a low profile.'

'What about that man from the photograph?'

'No one answering to that description has spoken to her. She did some shopping on Monday night but, apart from that, all she's done is work. But then I've told you all that. She leaves the house each day at seven and returns each evening at seven. She has made no stops, she's had no visitors.'

'Right.' Nicholas drummed his fingers against the desk.

'Oh, except tonight—she asked your chauffeur to drop her off at a chemist shop.'

'That's hardly earth-shattering, is it?' Nicholas murmured dryly. 'OK, thanks, Keith.' Putting down the phone, he reached into a drawer and took out the ring box.

It was now just over a month until Cat's birthday. The business trip to Switzerland couldn't have come at a worse time. He hadn't wanted to leave her; in fact, he'd thought about taking her with him but he'd known what her answer would be. She kept insisting that her work was her priority in life! And getting her to come away with him and sit around while he dealt with his business wouldn't have been a smart move right now. The closer he tried to reel her in, the more she pulled away. That was when he had decided that maybe reverse psychology was needed. If he left her alone for a week, maybe it would give her time to reflect on their relationship. The passion between them was red-hot. She was bound to miss him!

It had been a risky strategy so close to her birthday so he'd given his PI rigid instructions to monitor her every move and contact him if anything unusual happened.

Even so, two days into his business trip he'd woken in a cold sweat in the middle of the night. He'd dreamed of Cat walking down the aisle of a church. She'd been wearing a long white dress and she had looked so breathtakingly beautiful that he had been filled with desire. She'd looked up and smiled—it was that special smile that she gave him sometimes when he reached to take her hand—but the smile hadn't been for him; it had been for the man in the photograph, the man her brother had set her up with! He'd woken in a complete state of shock!

That was when he'd decided that now was a bad time to be so far away from her. Important trip or not, he must have been an idiot going to Switzerland when he had so much more to lose in London. Cancelling the rest of his schedule, he'd flown back immediately. He'd felt a bit better, knowing that he was just a short drive away from her. So he'd held his nerve and kept his distance for a few days longer, phoning the PI for constant updates. But today he'd had enough. Five days was enough breathing space. He needed to wrap this up. He would propose tonight.

The ring was a spectacular solitaire; he was sure she would take one look at it and say yes. After all, marriage to him would solve all her financial problems. Not only would she claim her inheritance, but also she would bag a wealthy husband. In true McKenzie style, she wouldn't be able to resist. He wouldn't mention the fact that he wanted her to sign a prenuptial contract until just before the big day—by which time she wouldn't want to back down because she wouldn't want to lose her inheritance. It would all work out fine.

He heard the lift doors opening in the lounge area and put the ring in his jacket pocket before walking out to greet her.

But, to his surprise, his chauffeur was alone in the room.

'Where is she?' Nicholas glanced into the lift as if Cat might be hiding somewhere.

'Sorry, Mr Zentenas, but Ms McKenzie wanted me to drop her home. She said to tell you thank you for the lift and that she would phone you tomorrow.'

For a moment Nicholas was completely nonplussed. Even though Cat had told him on the phone that she didn't want to see him tonight, he hadn't really taken her seriously. 'What's she playing at?' He spoke more to himself than the driver.

'I don't think she is playing at anything, sir. She was wet through from the rain and—'

'I need to go over there and sort this out,' Nicholas murmured, a look of determination on his face.

Cat had just had a shower and put on a T-shirt and a pair of shorts that she wore for bed when her front doorbell rang. She frowned and looked at the clock. It was almost ten.

Putting the door on the catch, she swung it open a few inches and peered around the edge. She was surprised to see Nicholas standing outside. He looked very attractive in a dark suit and a pale blue shirt open at the neck.

'Hi!' she murmured distractedly. How did he manage to look both businesslike and overwhelmingly sexy? she wondered as her heart did a strange leap of pleasure.

'Hello.' He smiled. 'Are you going to let me in?'

'Oh! Yes.' She closed the door and then looked down at her clothing; if she had thought for one moment he might come over, she would have put something more glamorous on. But it was too late to do anything about it now, so she unfastened the chain before swinging the door open again. 'What are you doing here, Nicholas?'

'I wanted to see you. I thought I made that clear when I sent my driver over.'

'But I thought I made it clear that I wasn't up to seeing you tonight.' Her pleasure at seeing him turned to annoyance. He had no right to come over here laying down ultimatums. He didn't own her!

He closed the door. 'Catherine, it's been five days and I think that is quite long enough for you to be rested and ready for me.'

'I beg your pardon?' She put one hand on her hip and her eyes flashed fire at him. 'I think maybe you'd better just go.'

He smiled. 'I'd almost forgotten how much that temper of yours excites me.'

'And I had almost—but not quite—forgotten how arrogant you are.'

He smiled and his eyes took in the heat of annoyance on her high cheekbones and the soft curve of her lips, before moving lower to see the way her T-shirt clung to her curves and the white shorts revealed long, shapely golden brown legs. She was achingly gorgeous.

He reached out and took hold of her hand to pull her a little closer to him.

'Nicholas, I—'

The pressure of his lips against hers cut off her words. But it was a surprisingly tender kiss and it instantly made all her reservations start to crash down around her. Before she could help herself, she was kissing him back with equal tenderness and then suddenly the kiss changed from gently provocative to hungrily possessive.

She wanted him so much, had missed him so much. She lifted her hand up to stroke against his face. She loved the taut feel of his skin, the slightly rough bristle of his jaw line, the silky softness of his thick dark hair.

'You are so beautiful.' He breathed the words against her ear as his hands moved under her T-shirt to caress the warm silk of her naked skin. 'I've missed this…' His lips trailed down over her neck, his hands stroking over the firm curve of her breast, his fingers finding the hard aching peaks of her nipples.

'Missed *me*—don't you mean?' Even through the delirium of need that he stirred up inside her, she was aware that the sentence wasn't enough. She pulled back and looked up at him questioningly.

A man could drown in those sensual green eyes, he thought hazily. 'Missed *you* like crazy,' he murmured softly.

She smiled at him then. 'Well, that's OK, then.'

'Yes, I think it is.' Pulling the T-shirt up over her head, he tossed it on the floor.

He smiled and then, before she realized his intention, he lifted her up over his shoulder and carried her through towards her bedroom.

It was the first time she had made love with him in her own bed and it seemed strange somehow, seeing him surrounded by the familiarity of her own things. The scatter cushions on her bed were well and truly scattered; the old teddy bear that was of sentimental value because it had been a last Christmas gift from her mother was similarly dispatched.

She arched her back against the cool sheets and invited his touch, his lips, his body.

'I don't know what you do to me.' He growled the words as he ripped off his jacket and started to unbutton his shirt.

She smiled at the words. Yes, Nicholas held control of her but she had a certain power over him as well. The knowledge was delicious; it made her feel as if everything was going to be OK, that the untamed seducer could be won over.

They were foolish thoughts but when they were together like this she allowed them full rein.

Naked, he joined her in the deep comfort of the double bed. He kissed her all over, luxuriating in the warmth of her responses. Because it was five days since he had made love to her, his pleasure seemed heightened and he had difficulty holding back. Every sinuous movement of her hips brought him closer to climax. It took all his self-control to tease her a little—torment her with his tongue, make her gasp his name.

Only when she begged him for release did he allow himself to let go. But even then, after taking her and pleasuring her and feeling the thrill of completion, when he pulled her close he wanted her all over again.

He could feel her heart beating against his chest as if she had been running a race, could smell the fresh scent of shampoo in her hair as he nuzzled against the silky blonde tresses.

'That was incredible,' he breathed softly against her ear and kissed the side of her face. She smiled a sleepy happy smile.

'Tell me about Switzerland,' she murmured, cuddling closer.

'Switzerland? Why do you want to know about that?'

'I'm just interested in how your days have been filled since I saw you last.'

There was something ingenuous about the statement and he felt a wash of shame that he had lied to her about staying away so long. 'There is not much to tell. It was just business.' He stared up at the ceiling and wondered what the hell was the matter with him.

'There must be something to tell. Was it snowing? Were the women very beautiful?'

'No, it wasn't snowing. The women, well...' He shrugged. 'I didn't have much time to look at the women, to be honest.'

She closed her eyes. All week she had been imagining him with incredibly sophisticated and gorgeous women, having dinner with them—making love to them. It had almost driven her out of her mind. She hated herself for being foolish enough to care.

But she did care. She cared about everything where he was concerned. 'Well, if there's not much to tell about Switzerland—tell me about Crete,' she invited softly.

'You know what Crete is like—you've been there.' She certainly had been there, he reminded himself staunchly. Between them, the McKenzie clan had pulled quite a scam.

'No, I mean what is it like where you live? What is your house like?'

'Why do you want to know about that?' His eyes held a certain coolness that struck at her.

'I was just curious, but it doesn't matter.' She pulled away from him.

He caught hold of her hand and drew her back before she could move too far away. 'Why are you curious? You don't usually ask me things.'

She allowed him to pull her back into his arms. She didn't ask him things because she was afraid that the closer she got to him, the harder it would be to ignore the fact that she was crazy about him. 'I don't know why I asked. It's just that I always see you in the impersonal surroundings of your hotel suites.'

He stroked her hair back from her face. 'I know, why don't I take you to my house in Crete for the weekend?' It would be the perfect place to propose to her, he thought suddenly. Plus it would get her away from her father, who would be arriving back soon.

'Don't be silly, Nicholas.' She pulled away from him with a frown. 'Why would you do that?'

'Why do you think?' He looked at her mischievously, one dark eyebrow raised.

'Because we can have an uninterrupted weekend of sex.'
She supplied the words dryly.

'Plus you can check out my décor,' he teased. 'Find out if
I favour the minimalist look or not.'

'Ha ha, very funny.'

He watched as she swung away from him and reached to
pick up her shorts from the floor. 'Do you want a drink or
something?' She flicked him a glance over her shoulder.

She was running away from him again. Why did she keep
doing this? He'd never met a woman who was so passionate
and yet so... hard to fathom and pin down.

'It's very warm in Crete at the moment—twenty-eight
degrees. You can relax by the pool, recharge your batteries.'
He made the tempting offer and then stared at her back in frustration when she didn't answer immediately.

'Actually, I'm busy this weekend.'

'Busy doing what?'

She looked around at him with a raised eyebrow. 'Just
busy, you know. Catching up on work.' She opened a drawer
and took out another T-shirt and pulled it over her head. 'But
thanks for the offer.' She was heading for the door now. 'Did
you say whether you'd like a drink or not? I'm going to put
the kettle on.'

'I'll have a coffee.'

'OK.' She smiled at him breezily and then closed the door
behind her.

Nicholas stared up at the ceiling. *Busy this weekend.* The
words taunted him. What was she going to do—meet up with
her father...meet up with the man from the photograph?

He threw back the sheet and reached for his clothes. She had
to come to Crete and preferably for longer than just a weekend.

'Listen, Cat, I've been thinking—' As he strode into the
other room he was surprised to see her sitting on the sofa, her

head down between her knees. 'Are you all right?' He moved over towards her hurriedly.

'Yeah, I'm fine. I'm just tired and I was waiting for the kettle to boil.'

He crouched down in front of her to look at her. 'You don't look fine. You look very pale.'

'Really, don't fuss, Nicholas. I'm fine.' She pushed him away and went over to the kitchen to continue making their drinks.

He watched her with a frown.

'So what were you thinking about?' she prompted him firmly. She didn't want to talk about what could be wrong with her.

Her hand shook as she lifted up the jar of coffee. She was almost frightened to unscrew the cap again because a few moments ago the aroma had made her stomach suddenly heave.

'Are you sure you are OK?'

His voice seemed to be coming from a long way away.

'Yes—just tired.' It took all her willpower to get herself a glass of water from the tap.

'Do you want me to make the coffee?'

She nodded. 'Actually—yes, thanks, Nicholas.' It was a relief to get away from the situation.

Cat went into the bathroom and closed the door.

It was strange; she had always liked the smell of coffee before. But then she had heard that pregnancy could affect the senses like that. Surely she couldn't be pregnant? The idea pounded through her. Yes, they had made love once in Venice without any protection. But it had just been once! How unlucky would it be that the first time she made love she got pregnant? The odds against that would be high—surely?

She opened up the bathroom cabinet and found the pregnancy testing kit. She'd been too anxious to use it earlier but she couldn't put it off any longer—she needed to know the truth.

Nicholas put the coffee down on the lounge table just as Cat's mobile started to ring. He picked it up from the sofa and glanced at the screen. He could see that the call was from her father.

He quickly switched the phone off and then slipped it down under the cushions. Carter McKenzie could go to hell.

'I was thinking that we could make it a long weekend in Crete,' he said as Cat returned a little while later. She still looked very pale, he noted. 'You know you could do with a break. You do look a bit tired.'

'Yes, I think maybe you should go now.' She pulled a hand distractedly through her long blonde hair.

Was she agreeing to go to Crete? Was she even listening to him? He frowned. Maybe her mind was running ahead, thinking about meeting up with her father—thinking about a marriage of convenience?

'There are things we need to discuss,' he said firmly.

She gave him a strange look. 'Like what?'

'Like you taking some time off work next week.'

'It's too busy at the office right now to even contemplate taking time off.'

'I would have thought that discussing the Zentenas contract would give you complete freedom to be out of the office.'

'But we wouldn't be discussing the contract.' She shook her head. She couldn't think about this right now; her head was all over the place.

'We *could* discuss it,' he said softly. 'Amongst other things.'

She shook her head. He was teasing her now and she couldn't take it. 'Look, Nicholas—I'm really not in the mood for this right now.'

She wasn't in the mood to talk about work? He looked at her in perplexity.

Cat suddenly noticed the probing way he was watching her and tried to turn away from him, but he reached out a hand and pulled her back.

'Are you feeling ill?'

'No!' She tried to stop him but he pulled her closer and tipped her face upwards so that he could look at her closely.

'I'm fine.' She closed her eyes and then shivered with desire when he stroked his fingers over the side of her face.

'You've been putting in too many hours in that office.'

His voice was huskily concerned and her eyes flew open to meet his. He looked concerned as well—but it was an illusion, of course. He wasn't really bothered about her. He just had some free time at the weekend and thought he'd spend it making love.

'Come to Crete with me for the weekend, Catherine. I know you said you are busy, but surely whatever it is can wait?'

When she didn't answer him, he pulled her closer into his arms. She allowed herself to be held. It felt wonderful and she closed her eyes, trying desperately to think sensibly about what she should do.

What would he say if she told him she was pregnant? The question sizzled through her. He would probably finish with her immediately! But then she didn't know for sure how he would react, a little voice whispered insidiously inside her. She didn't even know for sure how she felt right now—she supposed she was in shock.

'A little time alone together would be fun,' he said softly as he stroked her hair back from her face. 'Don't you think?'

Maybe a weekend in his company would help her decide what she should do? And, if nothing else, it would give her a chance to recharge her batteries and think.

'I suppose it would.' Her voice was muffled against his chest.

He smiled. 'So, pack a bikini and I'll pick you up tomorrow morning, early—say seven.'

She was allowing him to take over. But really she didn't have a lot of strength left to argue. 'And we could talk about the contract?' she managed vaguely as he pulled away from her.

He smiled at that. 'On Monday we will talk about the contract.'

'I have to be back in the office on Monday.'

'We'll see.'

'No, I *really* have to be back by Monday morning.'

He nodded and reached for his jacket. 'Get some sleep and I'll see you bright and early tomorrow.'

CHAPTER TWELVE

HEAT danced like shimmering water on the tarmac road.

Ahead, through the haze, Cat could see the blue glimmer of the sea. She couldn't believe that she was back in Crete, that she was pregnant or that she was here with Nicholas Zentenas. As she sat next to him in the open-top Jeep, her mind was bouncing in much the same way as the vehicle had a few moments ago over some of the potholed lanes.

It was all happening too fast. She didn't know what to think. But she was already starting to regret coming here. As soon as the private jet had landed an hour ago on the runway, the memories of Crete had started and now they were competing for space along with everything else she had to reflect on.

'Here we are; this is my home.' Nicholas drove the car around the curve of the bay. Up ahead, a white villa gleamed bright in the sunshine; perched like a wedding cake in three tiers, it looked down over an olive grove towards a stunning white beach.

Pink oleander lined the driveway and the gardens were tropically lush, thanks no doubt to a robust sprinkler system. Red bougainvillea was twined over the carport and a turquoise pool sparkled against the greenery, sun-beds and parasols laid out in invitation.

'It's a beautiful place,' Cat remarked as they stepped out of the vehicle.

'I like it.' He took her overnight bag from the back of the car and led the way up to the front door.

No expense had been spared inside the villa and the furnishings were exquisite but to Cat's surprise it also had a homely lived-in feel with the trinkets of everyday life scattered around. She glanced at the family photographs as she followed him through towards the master bedroom and made a note to go back and study them in more detail later.

Like the rest of the house, the bedroom was luxurious but it was the spectacular views along the coast from large sliding glass doors that held her attention.

'Its lovely that the coastline is unspoilt.' She walked across to look out. 'So many scenic places seem to be turning into concrete jungles these days, with no regard for beauty or wildlife.' She reached to slide the door open. The air was hot and silent except for the distant sound of the waves breaking on the shore below. 'I hate the way some developers destroy our environments under the guise of progress.'

'So do I.' Nicholas watched her with a frown. He wanted to remind her that her father was one of those people but he bit the words back. Did she just lie to herself? he wondered. Or was she simply blinded by love for her family?

And, if that was the case, did that make her a bad person? Suddenly he didn't think so. He swept a hand through the darkness of his hair, wondering if once again he was looking for excuses to justify her behaviour. The trouble was that these kind of doubts had been plaguing him for a while now—in fact, ever since spending time with her in Venice he was finding it harder and harder to see her in any kind of cold and calculating light.

She turned and he quickly composed himself. 'I think it's time for lunch. Are you hungry?'

'Maybe—a little.'

He nodded. 'I'll go and throw something together in the kitchen. Make yourself at home.'

When he left the room Cat changed out of her jeans and put on a red bikini and a matching pair of shorts with a cropped white T-shirt. Then she padded barefoot outside to dip a toe into the turquoise water of the pool and admire the garden. When she walked back up towards the house she saw Nicholas through an open door that led through from the kitchen on to the terrace.

She leaned against the doorframe and watched him for a moment whilst he was unaware of her presence. It was strange seeing him in this domesticated setting; he seemed so relaxed, and even more attractive if that was at all possible.

'Need some help?' she asked as he turned and saw her.

'No, I was just making a salad.'

'What, without a chef?' she teased him. 'Are you sure you can manage without that team of staff who usually cater to your every whim?'

'Highly amusing, Catherine!' He smiled. 'If you are going to make fun, you may as well make yourself useful. Come in here and cater to a few of my whims.'

'Sounds interesting.'

'I can make it very interesting.' He caught hold of her as she stepped through the doorway and pulled her into his arms to kiss her. It was a hard yet intimately satisfying kiss and at the same time he was pulling her T-shirt off.

'Nice bikini,' he growled as he drew back to look at her. The ring of his mobile phone interrupted them. 'Damn!' He frowned. 'That might be important—I'm expecting to close a deal this weekend.'

'You'd better answer the call, then.' Cat smiled at him and broke away to carry on where he had left off making the salad.

She half listened as he talked in Greek to whoever was at the other end of the line. The conversation was about donating money for the building of a new orphanage. She remembered she had heard him talking about this before and had doubted her translation. But now it seemed she had been right the first time and Nicholas was involved with the charity in a big way.

He had to be a nice person to do something like that—a person who cared about people, about children, not just about the business of making money.

He finished the call and then went over to stand behind her as she rinsed some leaves under the cold water in the sink. He slipped one hand around her waist and kissed the side of her neck. She felt like melting against him.

It was nice being with him like this. It felt as if they were a real couple.

'I like having you here in my house.'

'Do you?'

'Yes, and you are good in the kitchen—you look like you really know what you are doing with that colander.'

'You're just getting your own back now for my earlier remark.' She laughed.

He kissed the side of her neck again. 'But I'm serious when I tell you that I like having you here.'

'You just like *having* me.' She tried to sound flippant but his hand was resting on the flatness of her stomach, stirring up all kinds of emotions inside her.

She allowed herself to daydream for a moment that she had told him about the baby and that he was delighted and excited and that they were going to prepare for the child together and that they would be a family.

She did want this baby. The realization was suddenly very strong. The emotional response to the tender way Nicholas was holding her, his hand resting almost protectively over her stomach, made her eyes blur with tears.

But she also wanted Nicholas. Throughout her relationship with him she had been wary—had feared putting her trust in him because ultimately her experience had taught her that men only let you down. But perhaps she hadn't given Nicholas a fair chance. Maybe she should have allowed her feelings full rein, because she had fallen in love with him. As hard as she tried to fight it, the truth was indisputable—she was head over heels about him. It was why she hadn't been able to finish with him; it was why she was standing here crying.

She blinked away the tears fiercely. Feeling emotional wasn't going to help. Maybe she should tell him about the baby and see what he said.

His mobile phone started to ring again.

'Sorry about this.' He pulled away from her.

'That's OK,' she said lightly. 'I had to leave without my phone this morning as I couldn't find it. Maybe it's a good thing.'

'Yes, they are a distraction.' He took the call and then moved out of the room to talk to whoever it was.

Cat laid the table outside on the terrace and then sat down to wait. The minutes ticked away and she helped herself to a few lusciously juicy black olives and poured herself a glass of iced water as she tried to work out exactly how to word her news. *Nicholas, I've got something to tell you...* No, maybe more direct. *Nicholas, I'm pregnant and I'm keeping the baby. If you don't want to be involved, then that's fine...I can manage on my own.*

She probably could manage on her own—somehow. But she didn't want to. And it wasn't the fact that money would be tight—it was far more than that. It was the emotional pull of her feelings for Nicholas. She longed for the intimacy they had shared today, standing in that kitchen. They had just been a few snatched moments within a web of moments but they had clarified something. She didn't want to be an island any more—she didn't want not to trust him. Life could be so much better than that.

What was taking Nicholas so long? Impatiently she scraped her chair back from the table and went to look for him. She could hear his voice; as usual, he was talking in his native tongue and the deep, attractive tone resonated down the hallway.

'Whether or not I use the inheritance money, I will still be funding the orphanage.'

The words made Cat's confident footsteps falter. Why was Nicholas talking about inheritance money? *He couldn't possibly be talking about her inheritance money, could he?* Confusion raced within her.

'I just want us to be clear about that,' Nicholas continued crisply. 'Time is of the essence now. I need everything in place before the end of the month.'

It was her birthday soon and Nicholas's words held the hallmarks of something her father and half-brother would say. Suddenly it was as if the cold from the tiled floor was striking through her, hitting her heart, draining all the warmth and life from her body. Did Nicholas know her family? Was he working in conjunction with them to get her inheritance? It wouldn't be the first time her brother had tried such an idea.

But why would a billionaire like Nicholas be interested in a scam like that? He didn't need money—it didn't make sense.

She must have got this wrong; there must be another explanation. Maybe her Greek was rustier than she had thought. Cat started to walk forward again and, as she rounded the corner, she could see Nicholas sitting behind a desk in a book-lined room. 'No, Demetrius, I'm going to play it safe, so I still want you to email the prenuptial agreement to me.' He smiled at her as she approached and just continued with his conversation. Obviously he presumed that she couldn't understand Greek.

'And as I said before, I want to marry her as soon as possible—preferably before the end of the month.'

There was no ambiguity about that statement and Cat felt the coldness inside her turn to the searing white heat of fury. There was a ringing in her ears and a surge of adrenalin that was truly scary. She didn't fully understand what was going on here but one thing was clear—Nicholas was setting up some kind of honey trap. He was using her—deceiving her. There was no difference between him and all the other men in her life. She felt sick with the knowledge.

'OK, Demetrius, I've got to go. I'll ring you later.' He put the phone down. 'Sorry to be so long, Catherine.' He switched to English with fluid ease.

She didn't answer him immediately—her brain was racing as she wondered how she should play this.

'Are you all right? You look a bit pale.'

The phoney concern was the last straw. 'Oh, yes, I'm fine, Nicholas.' Her voice was brittle.

'Good, well, let's relax and have some lunch—'

'Actually, why don't you just ask me now?'

'Ask you what now?'

'Ask me to marry you, of course, and get it over with.'

He leaned back in his chair and said nothing. Silence stretched between them, as tense as an elastic band drawn back as far as it could go and almost at breaking point. She could almost see his brain ticking over. 'What makes you think I'm going to ask you to marry me?'

'What makes you think that I don't understand Greek?' She switched to his native tongue and watched his expression darken.

'I didn't know you spoke my language,' he said quietly.

'Oh, I'm well versed in your language.' Her voice was

scathing. 'But I'm not talking about Greek now. I'm talking about the language of deceit. I take it you and my father and half-brother are in on this together.' Her voice held a catch that was painful. She suddenly wanted to cry but she was damned if she would do that in front of him. She hated him—hated him with a fervency that she had never known before. She wanted to smack his smug arrogant face. But she just stood there, her hands curled into tight helpless fists at her sides.

He frowned. 'Why would you think I'm in on anything with your father and brother?'

'You must think I'm really stupid.'

'I don't think that for one minute, Catherine. And I can assure you that I am not in on anything with—'

'Don't bother to try and lie your way out of this, Nicholas. I can see the resemblance. You are just like them. All my life I have put up with their deceit and their lies as they used me to get what they wanted—namely money. I've endured their cold-hearted scheming. I've tried to fix the dreadful scams they have pulled. I even came back here to Crete last year to try and pay back money that they had conned out of unsuspecting people!' Her voice splintered with feeling.

Something changed in the darkness of his eyes as he looked at her. 'I didn't know—'

'Oh, for heaven's sake, save it, Nicholas!' She cut across him fiercely. 'I was actually starting to think that you were different. I can't believe that you took me in; I can't believe that I haven't seen it before. Because in reality you are just like them.'

'I'm nothing like them.' His voice was vehement.

'Well, at least you are no longer trying to pretend that you don't know them.'

The contempt in her voice lashed over him and suddenly he felt utterly ashamed for all the times he had tried to convince himself that she was scheming and conniving and just like her family. One thing was suddenly abundantly clear—he couldn't have been more wrong.

'What I can't understand is why.' Her voice softened and for a second her anger receded like the tide, giving a glimpse of raw pain in the green depths of her eyes. 'You don't need the money and yet you were prepared to use me like…like some kind of pawn in a game.'

The knowledge that he had misjudged her and hurt her like this was almost unbearable. He stood up from his chair. He needed to take her into his arms; he needed to try and explain that what she had overheard wasn't what it seemed—yes, his affair with her had started out as just a plan for revenge—but his feelings for her had changed and grown so much that he hadn't wanted to go through with that. *He needed to make her see that he loved her!* 'Catherine, we can sort this out.'

'I don't think so!' Her anger rushed back with the force of a tidal wave and blindly she reached and swept the papers from his desk. Files and papers spilled at her feet and amongst them she could see photographs of her, photographs taken as she was shopping and as she was walking into the building where she worked.

She bent down to pick one up with shaking hands. It was a snap of her having coffee with a work colleague, taken almost six months ago, certainly well before she had met Nicholas.

'You bastard!' Her voice was no more than a whisper. 'You had me followed as you made your plans—or did Michael do that? It's one of his little specialities—selling unsavoury ideas with a colour photo or two. He's been hounding me for ages to get married, using tactics just like that.'

'Catherine, I am not in league with your family.' He started to come around towards her.

'Keep away from me.' She backed towards the door.

'Just let me explain.'

'Explain what? How you seduced me to get your hands on the McKenzie money? What were you thinking when you were making love with me? Were you closing your eyes and thinking about how you would dupe me into putting the inheritance money into a joint bank account once we were married?'

'No, I wasn't thinking that.'

She didn't believe him. 'I don't care anyway.' Her chin slanted up as she met his eyes fiercely. 'Making love didn't mean anything to me—*you* don't mean anything to me.'

But she was lying. Even as she looked at him and hated him she still felt her heart twist with desire—with feelings for him that were so deep that they cut. Tears prickled perilously close to the surface and she swallowed them down hastily, furious with herself. 'I suppose you asked me here thinking that the lure of beautiful surroundings would act as a smoke-screen when you asked me to marry you—would make up for the fact that you have no feelings for me whatsoever. Well it wouldn't have worked.' She almost spat the words at him. 'Because my answer would still have been no; I would never have married you. Never.'

'Catherine, let's calm down and talk about this.' His voice was unwavering and rational and somehow that just made everything worse. He didn't need to calm down—he was perfectly in control because he didn't give a damn.

'Go to hell, Nicholas.' She turned and headed blindly down the hallway towards the front door.

'Where are you going?'

She was vaguely aware that Nicholas was calling after her but she ignored him and kept on going out of the front door and down on to the drive. She had no idea where she was going. All she knew was that she had to get away from him before she broke down into a million pieces. She may have foolishly lost her heart to him but she was damned if she was going to lose her pride as well.

The sun seared down on her from a clear azure sky. The only sound was the waves on the shore and the insistent hum of the cicadas. She wore no shoes and she was just in her bikini top and shorts with no sunscreen, but she didn't care. The heat of the road was burning the soles of her feet so she walked instead along the rough parched grass.

The sound of a car coming along the road behind her made her quicken her pace and start to run; that was when she caught her foot on the uneven ground and tumbled down. The fall winded her and for a second she couldn't move.

'Catherine, are you OK?' She heard a car door slam and a few seconds later Nicholas was crouching down beside her. 'Have you hurt yourself?'

'Go away.' She rubbed at her ankle; her eyes were blurred with tears and she couldn't even look at him.

'Come on, let's get you back to the house.' He touched her shoulder and she flinched.

'Leave me alone, Nicholas.'

'I know you are angry with me and you have every right to be.' His voice softened. 'But I can't leave you here. You've hurt yourself. You are miles from even the nearest village.'

She bit down on her lip.

'Let me take you back to the house and we'll sort this out—we'll talk and—'

'We *can't* sort this out, Nicholas.' She looked up at him then and her eyes were shadowed with emotion. 'I'm not one of your business deals that's gone wrong.'

'If it's any consolation, I never thought of you as a business deal.'

'You're right—it's no consolation. And I don't want to go

back to your house. I wouldn't go back there if it was the last
building left standing.'

Cat struggled to get onto her feet and that was when the
world seemed to tip and tilt on its axis as dizziness set in.
'Nicholas…' She breathed his name in panic before the world
just blacked out.

CHAPTER THIRTEEN

NICHOLAS'S voice seemed to be coming from a long distance away yet when she opened her eyes he was holding her close. She could smell the scent of his cologne, feel the heat of his body against hers.

She tried to think straight but the world felt fuzzy.

'Catherine, are you all right? Talk to me.' He stroked a hand along the side of her cheek and the tender touch made her recoil instantly.

'You passed out.'

'I know I passed out; just get away from me.'

He totally ignored her and the next moment he was scooping her up into his arms and carrying her back towards his car.

'Put me down, Nicholas!' Although her anger and the need to get away from him were strong, she felt too weak to struggle and she was forced to give herself up to the indignity of leaning her head against his shoulder. 'I don't want to go back to your house.'

'I'm not taking you back to my house.'

Cat was vaguely aware that she was in the passenger seat of his car but it was as if the journey was happening to someone else; she felt strangely detached and she just wanted to close her eyes and sleep.

She opened her eyes as he pulled up outside a white-washed house with blue shutters which were closed to the heat of the day.

'Where are we?'

'My cousin's house—she's a doctor. She can check you over.'

'I don't want to be checked over!' She felt panic and anger in equal measures now. 'Look, Nicholas, just take me to the airport. I want to go home.'

He ignored the request and instead came around to open the passenger door and lift her out. Once again she was forced to hold on to him as he strode down the path towards the front door.

The house was blissfully cool and dark inside. A woman appeared almost immediately and began talking in rapid Greek. Nicholas explained that Cat was a friend of his and that she had fallen and then blacked out.

A *friend*! The word clawed at Cat, inflaming her anger against him all over again.

They weren't friends—they weren't even lovers. Nicholas had used her. He was an enemy—a traitorous, calculating enemy who had tricked his way behind her defence mechanisms.

She pushed against his shoulder, her hands ineffectual against his powerful hold. 'I want you to let me go.'

'All in good time.'

'Place her on the sofa, Nicholas,' the woman ordered softly. 'Then you can leave us.'

As he put her down carefully and stepped back, perversely Cat felt bereft without his strength.

'Catherine?' The woman leaned closer. She spoke in English, her voice gentle and her manner soothing. 'Catherine, my name is Sophia Zentenas. I'm a doctor. Did you bang your head when you fell?'

'No. And I'm fine, really I am.' Cat struggled to sit up but as she tried the room felt as if it were spinning around.

'I think you should lie still, Catherine.' Sophia put a cool hand against her forehead. Then she checked her pulse rate. 'Your blood pressure is raised.'

'I'm not surprised,' Cat muttered wryly. 'Nicholas is enough to give anyone high blood pressure.'

Sophia laughed at that. 'You just lie still and I'll get my bag from the next room.'

Cat's eyes darted to Nicholas who was standing in the shadows. 'I want you to go now,' she told him firmly. 'I don't want you here.'

'I'm not going anywhere until I know you are all right.'

'It's over, Nicholas,' she told him calmly. 'Your little game has backfired. I suggest you take your phoney concern and tell my family that your plans have fallen through.'

'Catherine, I am not in league with your family.'

'I don't believe you.' She stared at him stonily. 'And anyway, you may as well be. You are as cold-blooded as they are.'

For a moment she thought she glimpsed a raw expression on his remote features.

'I didn't want to hurt you.'

'No, you just wanted to use me, steal the McKenzie money like they did—'

'I didn't need your money, Catherine.'

'Well, maybe that makes you worse than they are.' Her voice trembled. 'And that is stooping pretty low, believe me.'

There was a long silence. She could see a pulse moving on his jaw line.

'My father is a cheat and a liar and he has never really loved me.' She admitted the truth in a huskily broken tone. 'My half-brother is even worse, if that is possible. So I don't know what that makes you.'

'Catherine, why didn't you tell me this before?' He took a step closer and bent down beside her.

'Why would I tell you?' She practically spat the words at him. Her eyes blurred for a second. 'And anyway, would you want to admit to having a family like that?'

'Catherine, I'm so sorry,' He reached to touch her and she flinched.

'I want you to go.'

'I need to explain things. I wasn't going to take the money for myself. I was going to give it to a charity, to an orphanage—'

'I don't care what your plans were. I don't want to hear your explanations.'

'But I need to tell you—'

'Just leave me alone.' Her voice rose with distress. 'I don't want your excuses.'

'Nicholas, you'd better go.' Sophia's voice interrupted them gently. 'You are upsetting Catherine and I can't allow that. She needs to rest right now.'

For a second Nicholas hesitated and Cat thought that he was going to argue, but then he pulled back from her, his dark eyes shuttered. 'I'll wait in the other room.'

'No, I think it's best if you go home.' Sophia came closer. 'Catherine doesn't want you around. We'll ring you if you are needed.'

The curt dismissal wasn't something Nicholas would have accepted normally but, to Catherine's surprise, after a brief hesitation he nodded and with just a glance in her direction he strode out of the room.

As Sophia strapped a monitor on to Cat's arm to take her pulse they heard the sound of his Jeep starting up outside and then the roar of the engine as he sped away.

'There, feel better now?' Sophia asked softly.

Cat nodded and then bit down on her lip as tears flooded her eyes.

'My cousin has obviously hurt you a great deal, Catherine,' Sophia said briskly. 'And therefore he is not worth your tears—even if he is undeniably as handsome as the devil.'

Catherine smiled tremulously. 'Yes… It's just… I can't believe I've made such a terrible mistake. He's used me.'

Sophia frowned. 'I know it's not an excuse. But I sometimes think Nicholas has difficulty in trusting women. Certainly since his divorce he has avoided any deep and meaningful relationship. I think he's frightened of being hurt again.'

'Frightened?' Cat gave a bitter laugh. 'I don't think Nicholas is frightened of anything.'

'I know he does give that impression.' Sophia shrugged. 'But, believe it or not, he's been through a lot in his life. He's never taken things for granted the way I have.'

'What do you mean?' Cat asked curiously.

'Well, for instance, I always took for granted the unconditional love of my family but he never did. I think deep down he was always frightened that love would be snatched away from him. That hard outer shell he likes to present to the world is just a front.'

'You're right. I don't believe you.'

Sophia looked at her quizzically and Cat felt herself blush. 'Sorry—I know he's your cousin… It's just…' She trailed off helplessly.

'It's just that he's hurt you and you love him,' Sophia finished for her softly.

'No! I hate him.'

Sophia smiled. 'You blood pressure was slightly raised until I asked that question and then it almost shot off the scale.' She took the straps off Cat's arm. 'Try to relax. Tell me, have you any idea why you passed out?'

'No. It was hot and I was running.' She shrugged. 'I haven't eaten properly for a while. I keep being sick.'

'Are you pregnant?'

The direct question made Cat's blush deepen. There was a long silence and she made no reply.

'I'm a doctor, Catherine. Anything you say to me will be in confidence.'

Cat hesitated for a moment and then nodded.

'Right, if you've been sick a lot, you're probably dehydrated and your blood sugars are low. Combined with the heat, it could account for you passing out. I think what you need to do is drink lots of fluids and rest for a while.'

'I want to go home to London, but my passport and belongings are at Nicholas's house.'

'I don't think you are fit to travel anywhere today.'

'I can't go back to Nicholas!' Cat's voice rose slightly in panic.

'Don't worry. You can stay here. I have a spare room.'

'I can't impose on you like that!'

'Why not?' Sophia smiled at her. 'I'd say it was the least I can do after my cousin has upset you so much. Now, let's have a look at your ankle.'

Cat watched as Sophia knelt to carefully examine her foot. She liked this woman's no nonsense, but gentle approach. She was soothing to be around. She was probably about ten years older than Nicholas, but incredibly attractive. Her raven dark hair was shiny, her sloe-dark eyes warmed with laughter lines.

'I don't think you have broken anything, it's just a sprain,' she declared as she put Cat's foot down again. 'I'll get you a drink and then I'll help you to the bedroom and, when you're ready, I'll make you something to eat.'

The sound of children laughing woke Cat. She lay in the cool darkened bedroom listening to them playing in the front garden, and watched the floral curtains flutter as a breeze caught them.

Somewhere a church bell was chiming. It was early Sunday morning and she had surprised herself by sleeping through the night, even though she had been sure she would toss and turn.

Her mind went back to yesterday and the discovery of Nicholas's duplicity and once again her eyes filled with tears. He'd said he wasn't in league with her family, but she didn't know if she believed that or not—she couldn't get a handle on why he had deceived her. Hastily she brushed her tears away, it was her hormones making her cry, she told herself shakily. She didn't care why Nicholas had treated her so badly—the only thing that counted was the fact that she had found him out. And she now knew she could never trust him. Now she knew that he was another man just like Ryan Malone.

She pushed back the covers of the bed and reached for the clothes that Sophia had lent her. As she fastened the long skirt, her hand rested for a moment on her stomach and she remembered how Nicholas had held her yesterday, remembered the foolish dreams about telling him about the baby—about being a family.

Briskly she turned to make the bed. Thoughts like that had been crazy. She certainly had no intention of telling Nicholas about the baby now. What was the point? She didn't want him in her life and he didn't want her. He'd probably be horrified to learn she was pregnant and demand she had an abortion. A baby definitely wouldn't figure in the ruthless plans of a man who had deceived her so callously, who cared nothing for her.

Her eyes were suddenly blinded with tears again. He could go to hell, she told herself fiercely. Because she was glad that she was pregnant; she wanted this child and one loving parent was enough. She would give her baby all the love and support that had been missing in her own life—and she could do that without the help of any man.

The sound of a car pulling up outside made her hurry towards the window.

Outside in the blaze of the morning sun she saw Nicholas climb out of his Jeep. He looked tall and handsome and her heart twisted instantly with pain.

She saw Sophia's two little girls running down the path to welcome him; they whooped for joy as he swung them up in his arms and whirled them around, they clamoured for more as he set them down again.

'Not now, girls.' His voice drifted up to the open window. 'I've come to see Catherine. How is she today?'

'OK, but Mummy says we are not to disturb her.'

'Is that so?' Nicholas glanced up and suddenly their eyes connected and it was as if an electric current passed between them. She dropped the curtain and stepped away from the window, her heart racing.

Hurriedly she moved to open the bedroom door, just as Sophia rushed up the stairs.

'Nicholas is here,' she hissed. 'What do you want me to tell him?'

'Tell him I can't see him,' Cat implored. 'I can't face him, Sophia.'

'All right, but he might not take no for an answer. He's phoned three times already and—'

'And you're right, I'm not going to take no for an answer.' Nicholas's deep tone cut across the conversation. Cat glanced around. He was coming up the stairs, a look of determination on his handsome features.

'Nicholas, I don't want to talk to you.' She took an instinctive step backwards into the bedroom. Her gaze swung to

Sophia beseechingly but it was too late—Nicholas was sweeping past his cousin.

'Give us some time alone, Sophia,' he demanded curtly. 'We have things to sort out.'

The next moment he had stepped into the bedroom and closed the door behind him.

'Nicholas, I don't think there is anything more for us to say. I just want you to give me my passport so I can go home.' She was pleased at how cool and composed she sounded whilst inside her heart was turning over with sadness, with a longing for something that could never be—with anger like molten fire.

'You are not going anywhere until you've heard me out.'

'How dare you come barging in here, laying down the law like I owe you something?' She crossed her arms defensively over her chest as he moved closer. 'I don't owe you anything. And there is nothing left to talk about.'

'Well, I owe you something,' he said softly. 'I owe you an apology. I'm sorry I hurt you, Catherine—really I am.'

The softness of his tone made her defences waver alarmingly.

'The only thing that you are sorry about is the fact that I've found you out and you are not going to get your hands on the McKenzie inheritance.'

'This was never about money,' he said quietly.

'So what was it about, Nicholas?'

'It was about revenge—about the fact that your father cheated me in a business deal. He lied and deceived me in a most ruthless fashion and almost succeeded in ruining my reputation.'

Cat could feel her heart beating violently against her chest. 'So you thought you would bed me for your revenge?'

'When I found out about your inheritance, it did seem the perfect way to get revenge. I knew your father wanted to get his hands on that money—and yes, I'll admit I had no qualms at first about using you to get to him.' He watched how she flinched at that and he reached out to touch her arm.

'Get away from me.' She stepped back angrily, her eyes burning into his.

'I thought you were as bad as they were,' he continued softly. 'I thought you were in alliance with them when they worked their vicious scams. In particular I thought you helped in that con they played here in Crete. I had photographs from a private investigator backing up that assumption.'

'Yes, well, your private investigator got it wrong,' she blazed. 'In fact he couldn't have got it more wrong. I was as duped as the people here in Crete. I gave money in good faith to Michael for what I believed to be an honest business venture. He used it to set up a scam. By the time I realized what was going on, the damage had already been done.'

'But you bailed your brother out,' Nicholas stated firmly.

'No—I repaid what he had stolen, which is something totally different.'

'Yes…I realize now that I made a mistake about you. I'm sorry, Catherine.' His eyes held steadily with hers. 'Truly I am, sorry from the bottom of my heart.'

'You haven't got a heart.'

'That's where you are wrong.' He said the words quietly. 'The only problem was that I didn't trust myself enough to listen to it.'

'Don't try and sweet-talk me, Nicholas, because it won't work. I've met men like you before. Unbeknown to me, my brother set me up once before. I met someone I thought knew nothing about my background, someone who told me he loved me. I'd been going out with him for six months and I was starting to trust him—starting to have feelings for him—and then I discovered it was all an elaborate hoax, just so my family could get their hands on the McKenzie money. Do you know what a curse that inheritance is? Do you know what it feels like to have people lie to you, profess feelings they haven't got, just to get your money?'

'Surprisingly, yes, I do.' Nicholas's voice was grim and she remembered suddenly how Sophia had told her how difficult he had found it to trust women since his divorce.

'Well, then, maybe you should have been a little more careful with my emotions.' Quickly she shut out the feelings of sympathy.

'I never told you I loved you, Catherine.'

He noted how her complexion paled, how her eyes burnt like bright emerald fire.

'So what were you going to say when you got around to asking me to marry you?' She shot the question at him with a quiver in her voice. 'Come away with me so we can have red-hot sex on tap for ever?'

His lips twisted derisively. 'I don't know what I was going to say. To be honest, when I held you in my arms, revenge was far from my thoughts.'

'Liar.'

'It's the truth, Catherine. I started to have feelings for you that I didn't want to have—started to doubt my motives.'

'But you were still going to go through with your revenge until I overheard your little plan and ended it.'

'I was definitely going to ask you to marry me—yes. But whether I would have gone through with the revenge of taking the money—' He shrugged. 'I was having second thoughts about that.'

'It didn't sound to me as if you were having second thoughts. Why would you have asked me to marry you if you weren't going to take the money?'

He held her gaze steadily. 'That was a question I kept

asking myself over and over again and I kept ignoring the answer because, quite frankly, it scared the hell out of me.'

Cat stared at him as she tried to digest what he was saying to her, and then she shook her head. 'I don't believe that you were having second thoughts. You were having a prenuptial agreement drawn up when I overheard you talking on the phone.'

'Yes, I got my lawyer to draw up a prenuptial agreement as a safeguard. I wasn't sure I could trust my feelings where you were concerned. I admit that, having made a mistake once before in marriage, it's made me cynical and overcautious—it's made me doubt you when I really didn't want to doubt you. But I was sure that I wanted you. I still want you,' he said huskily. 'And I know now that I was wrong to ever believe for one moment that you are anything like your family.'

'I have to give you ten out of ten for being able to talk your way out of a situation, Nicholas,' she said fiercely. 'I suppose this is why you are so wealthy. You could persuade a person that the sun is made of butter and have them reaching to put some on their bread.'

'Well, good, because I'm asking you to marry me and I want very much for you to say yes.'

'You must think I'm very naïve.' Cat's voice trembled alarmingly. 'I wouldn't marry you if you were the last man left in the universe.'

'I'm asking you to marry me because I want you in my life, Catherine. I've fallen in love with you. The proposal has nothing to do with revenge,' he continued smoothly, as if she hadn't said anything.

Cat shook her head. 'I can't believe you've got the gall to go ahead with this proposal when I know you are lying.'

'I'm not lying. I don't want anything to do with the

McKenzie inheritance, Catherine—you've got to believe me. To be honest, it was only ever a drop in the ocean to me anyway. And the charity will still get its large donation from me.'

Cat turned away from him and stared out of the window. Her eyes were blurred with tears and she didn't want him to see her crying.

'I've behaved badly towards you, but I want you to know that my only real sin was not having the courage to believe my heart. I love you, Cat, please believe that.'

She didn't answer him—she couldn't—she was too choked up with emotion.

'And I do trust you,' he continued softly. 'I tore up the pre-nuptial agreement when it was emailed to me this morning. Everything I have is yours.'

'I don't want anything from you.'

'Cat, please forgive me.'

She shook her head and stood with her back resolutely to him.

'Do you see that land outside the window?' Nicholas asked suddenly. He reached past her to hold back the curtain.

Through the haze of her tears, she took in the gentle undulating landscape, the silver-green olive trees and the blaze of lemon groves against the backdrop of the sea.

'That land meant something to the people of this village. It meant something to the family who took me in. They trusted me to save it for them. I, in turn, trusted your father in a business deal. We had an agreement to preserve all of this. But he broke that deal. I went away and when I came back the land was torn up—the ancient trees that had been lovingly tended for generations had been torn apart—a way of life was under threat, with bulldozers and contractors everywhere. And people who had once treated me with respect—with love—looked at me once again as if I were a stranger.'

Cat wiped the tears from her cheeks. 'Well, I'm sorry, Nicholas—my father isn't a man to trust—it's a lesson I learnt a long time ago. He's hurt me too.'

'I realize that now.'

'At least you were able to put everything right again—the countryside looks unscathed—'

'Yes, but I didn't manage to do it before my adoptive father died. He didn't live to see how sorry I was. He died thinking I had let him down and that was the last thing in the world I would ever have wanted to do to him. My family here gave me everything and I'm not talking about money now—I'm talking about the important things in life like love and respect. I wanted so much to repay that debt.'

For a moment Cat remembered Sophia's words to her yesterday. About how Nicholas never took the love of his family for granted. That deep down he was always frightened that love would be snatched away from him. That the hard outer shell he liked to present to the world was just a front.

Things about Nicholas's character started to clarify in her mind. It had probably hit him very hard to think he had let down the family who had taken him in. 'I didn't know you were adopted,' she said quietly.

'It's not relevant.'

She brushed a shaking hand across her wet cheek and turned to look at him. 'It's obviously relevant. It was why you were giving that money to an orphanage—wasn't it? How long did you spend in one?'

'That's not important!'

Once more she could see the arrogant glint in his eyes, the proud tilt of his head. Nicholas had insecurities that he hid well. Sophia was right—she could see that now. Maybe he wasn't so different from her after all. They had both endured traumas in their childhood. They had both been hurt in adulthood and it had made them wary—too wary, perhaps. 'I'm sorry my father hurt you so much.'

The gentleness of her tone tore at Nicholas. 'It's not your fault. It was never your fault.'

Cat shrugged. 'I have a family I am ashamed of.'

'I'm ashamed of myself right now.'

'So you should be.' For a moment there was a gleam of humour amidst the pain in her eyes. 'But we can call it quits if you like,' she offered softly.

Nicholas raked a hand through his hair. He felt awkward—like a complete rat. 'It's more than I deserve.'

'That's true…' She smiled at him. 'But holding on to anger isn't good—we need to move on with our lives.'

He couldn't believe that he had ever doubted this woman's integrity. She was so gentle and honest and her family had hurt her so much in the past. That he had added to that pain was almost beyond endurance.

'Anyway, I need to get back to London, so if you would just bring me my passport…'

Nicholas watched as she tilted her head upwards, a determined look in her eyes.

He should have read the signs—should have known that she was nothing like them. But he had been so bound up in his quest for revenge—so tied up with guarding his heart in case he made another big mistake in marriage that he had almost made the biggest one of his life and let her get away.

'Cat, I don't want you to go,' he said quietly. 'I realize that it's going to take a lot to make you trust me again, but I'm willing to work at it. I meant what I said before. I love you very much and I want us to be together. No secrets—no hidden agenda. Just the two of us getting to know each other all over again.'

'I think it might be a bit late for that.'

'I don't accept that.' He moved closer towards her. 'You have feelings for me—I know that you do.'

The arrogance was back in his voice. 'Look at me and tell me honestly that you don't want me.' His voice was terse.

She looked up into his eyes and tried to find her voice but it seemed to have deserted her.

'You see you can't!'

'Nicholas, things aren't as simple as all that,' she breathed huskily.

'Things are as simple or as complicated as we choose to make them.' He reached out and pulled her into his arms and then he kissed her. It was a hard brutal kiss and yet so filled with passion that she found herself yielding to it immediately. It felt so good to be in his arms.

She still loved him…

'You see.' There was a gleam of triumph in his voice as he pulled back from her. 'You want me—it's as simple as that.'

'Not really.' She pulled away from him with a frown.

'Look, I know you are wary of me—I know I've messed up, but…'

'Nicholas, I'm pregnant.'

The words fell from her lips before she could stop them. 'It must have happened in Venice—that night—well…you know…'

There was a look of incredulity on his handsome features that would have struck her as amusing if she hadn't been so tense. This was the real test. It was all very well pretending to love her—whispering glib words about trust and want. But a baby—well, that wasn't something you could gloss over. It made everything real; it focused the mind and the emotions until there was no room for pretence.

'So you see it isn't just about you and me any more,' she carried on quickly. 'Which is another reason why we need to move on from anger and revenge and all of that. But don't worry. I don't want anything from you. I can manage on my own and—'

'How long have you known?'

'What?' She looked up at him in trepidation. 'Only a few days.'

'You should have told me…' He raked a hand through his hair. 'I've hurt you like this and you are pregnant! No wonder you passed out!'

'I'm all right now.'

'I'm so sorry, Catherine!'

The feeling in his voice and in his eyes wasn't something she could doubt. But she didn't want his sorrow.

'You are the best thing to happen to me in a long, long time.' He ran a hand tenderly along the side of her face, a look of wonder in his eyes. 'And now you are pregnant and, just when life couldn't be more perfect, I've nearly ruined it all.'

She frowned. 'Nicholas, you don't have to even pretend to want the baby—I said I can manage and I meant it.'

'What the hell are you talking about?' He grated the words out unevenly, his voice broken with the weight of his emotion. 'Of course I want the baby—and I want you. I can't think of anything I've ever wanted more in my whole life.'

She couldn't speak for a moment—she was too over-whelmed with the craziest feelings. Exhilaration—but also fear in case this too was some kind of test—some kind of cruel trickery—and that fate would snatch this away from her.

'Please give me a chance to prove my love to you and to our baby, Catherine… We can arrange a wedding for after your twenty-first birthday. I'm begging you not to walk away.'

And suddenly, as she looked up at his proud face, she knew in her heart that he meant what he was saying and that if she walked away from him without giving what they had a chance that she would regret it for the rest of her life.

'I love you, Nicholas,' she whispered softly.

'I love you too.' He pulled her into his arms, holding her tight, knowing he would never let her go.

HARLEQUIN *Presents*

THE MEDITERRANEAN PRINCES

Playboy princes, island brides—
bedded and wedded by royal command!

Roman and Nico Magnati—
Mediterranean princes with undisputed
playboy reputations!

These powerfully commanding princes expect their
every command to be instantly obeyed—and they're not
afraid to use their well-practiced seduction to get want
they want, when they want it....

Available in October

HIS MAJESTY'S MISTRESS
by Robyn Donald
#2768

Don't miss the second story in Robyn's brilliant duet,
available next month!:

THE MEDITERRANEAN PRINCE'S
CAPTIVE VIRGIN
#2776

REQUEST YOUR FREE BOOKS!

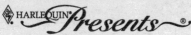 

2 FREE NOVELS PLUS 2 FREE GIFTS!

YES! Please send me 2 FREE Harlequin Presents® novels and my 2 FREE gifts (gifts are worth about $10). After receiving them, if I don't wish to receive any more books, I can return the shipping statement marked "cancel". If I don't cancel, I will receive 6 brand-new novels every month and be billed just $4.05 per book in the U.S. or $4.74 per book in Canada, plus 25¢ shipping and handling per book and applicable taxes, if any*. That's a savings of close to 15% off the cover price! I understand that accepting the 2 free books and gifts places me under no obligation to buy anything. I can always return a shipment and cancel at any time. Even if I never buy another book, the two free books and gifts are mine to keep forever.

106 HDN ERRW 306 HDN ERRL

Name	(PLEASE PRINT)

Address	Apt. #

City	State/Prov.	Zip/Postal Code

Signature (if under 18, a parent or guardian must sign)

Mail to the **Harlequin Reader Service:**
IN U.S.A.: P.O. Box 1867, Buffalo, NY 14240-1867
IN CANADA: P.O. Box 609, Fort Erie, Ontario L2A 5X3

Not valid to current subscribers of Harlequin Presents books.

Want to try two free books from another line?
Call 1-800-873-8635 or visit www.morefreebooks.com.

* Terms and prices subject to change without notice. N.Y. residents add applicable sales tax. Canadian residents will be charged applicable provincial taxes and GST. Offer not valid in Quebec. This offer is limited to one order per household. All orders subject to approval. Credit or debit balances in a customer's account(s) may be offset by any other outstanding balance owed by or to the customer. Please allow 4 to 6 weeks for delivery. Offer available while quantities last.

Your Privacy: Harlequin Books is committed to protecting your privacy. Our Privacy Policy is available online at www.eHarlequin.com or upon request from the Reader Service. From time to time we make our lists of customers available to reputable third parties who may have a product or service of interest to you. If you would prefer we not share your name and address, please check here. ☐

HP08R

MEDITERRANEAN DOCTORS

Demanding, devoted and
drop-dead gorgeous—
These Latin doctors will
make your heart race!

Smolderingly sexy Mediterranean doctors

Saving lives by day…red-hot lovers by night

**Read these four Mediterranean Doctors stories
in this new collection by your favorite authors,
available in Presents EXTRA October 2008:**

THE SICILIAN DOCTOR'S MISTRESS
by SARAH MORGAN

THE ITALIAN COUNT'S BABY
by AMY ANDREWS

SPANISH DOCTOR, PREGNANT NURSE
by CAROL MARINELLI

THE SPANISH DOCTOR'S LOVE-CHILD
by KATE HARDY

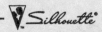

SPECIAL EDITION™

FROM *NEW YORK TIMES* BESTSELLING AUTHOR

LINDA LAEL MILLER

A STONE CREEK CHRISTMAS

Veterinarian Olivia O'Ballivan finds the animals in Stone Creek playing Cupid between her and Tanner Quinn. Even Tanner's daughter, Sophie, is eager to play matchmaker. With everyone conspiring against them and the holiday season fast approaching, Tanner and Olivia may just get everything they want for Christmas after all!

Available December 2008
wherever books are sold.